Deadly Facets

by *Sherrill Lewis*

Sherrill M. LEWIS

Book Three
Maggie Storm Blue Mystery

Shoppe Foreman Publishing
Guthrie, Oklahoma, USA

Published by

Shoppe Foreman Publishing

Guthrie, Oklahoma 73044 USA
www.ShoppeForeman.com

Cover watercolor by Bill Miller
Stillwater, Oklahoma

Printed in the United States of America
Printing/manufacturing information
can be found on the last page.

ISBN-13: 978-1517106096
ISBN-10: 1517106095

Dedication

My husband, Gene Lewis:
my beloved hero for thirty years now,
and forever after later.

Table of Contents

Acknowledgements

Thank you!

To my Lord, who continues to bless me with the ability to write pretty words, even when I am plotting mischief, mayhem, and murder scenes.

I appreciate always the many faithful readers who continue to buy my books.

My intrepid first readers who keep a stock of red pens handy: Gene Lewis, Judith Sexton, and Robert Parks, I could not do it without you. To the very talented cover artist, Bill Miller, who makes a beautiful cover in spite of my rough sketches. Last, but certainly not least, my publisher, Larry Foreman.

Sherrill M. Lewis

Disclaimer

Baywater County, Maine, does not exist. Baysinger Cove and all towns in that county are fictitious. People and events, for the most part, are products of the author's very overactive imagination.

1

Mariposa Crazy Cottage

A HARSH NOISE FROM SOMEWHERE OUTSIDE was carried on the chill of the damp and foggy afternoon in Baysinger Cove, Maine. Maggie Storm Blue glanced out the window toward The Happy Bookworm on the far side of Franklin Road.

She took a deep breath and turned her attention to the next customer waiting in line for her to cut trims. At ten o'clock this morning, November 12th, her very own Mariposa Crazy Cottage's "Open" sign had been turned on for the first time.

"What was that?" A woman with pure white, salon-perfect hair put a basket filled with spools of ribbons and trims on the cutting table. "Sounded like a car backfiring."

"Yankee Thrift" was more than an idiosyncratic phrase; it was a true watchword for many native New Englanders. People tended to keep their vehicles for decades, until duct tape, baling wire, rust, and chewing gum no longer held the antiquated beasts together. New technology had, for the most part, solved the emission problem, so it may have been old Hiram Beecham's irascible vintage jalopy sounding off its characteristic belching.

"Or a gunshot." Maggie was a voracious reader of cozy mysteries, so it was no surprise that her mind jumped to that

1

conclusion.

"Probably someone's taking potshots at the squirrels. Pesky varmints, especially when they get in the attic."

"How many yards?" Maggie asked her customer.

"Two yards of each of these, please."

Maggie scanned the barcode labels, printed the summary tape, and returned the cut trims to the customer's shopping basket. "Looks like you're next and my father will check you out."

The door chime rang, announcing yet another incomer. A woman in a full-length navy blue down-filled quilted coat stood smack-dab in the middle of the wide doorway and looked around. She lowered her hood and unbuttoned the top button. The light caught the facets of the beads in her necklace, and rainbows danced.

Nothing sparkles like real Swarovski. Maggie didn't much like Charlotte Morgan. To the woman's credit, however, Maggie conceded that she did have exquisite taste in jewelry.

"Where's Pattysue?" Charlotte demanded, glaring at Maggie.

"It's Wednesday. Her day at the bookstore." *As if you didn't know.*

Pattysue's mother-in-law snatched off her fuzzy red gloves, "I wish Pattysue would work for you full-time. She needs to get away from that *awful* bookstore. I cannot stand that Harold person. And there's that filthy crow squawking at the customers. Rude, too."

Maggie wondered what pithy remark that smart bird had thrown at Charlotte. Whatever it was, she was inclined to agree in principle since she did not like the woman at all.

Charlotte glanced up at the clock, turned on her designer-boot heel, stomped out the door, got in her car, and drove off.

Rod shook his head. "That woman is a piece of work."

"I can't put my finger on it, but I've disliked her from the minute I first met her."

A few minutes later, the front door slammed. Pattysue Morgan rushed in with tears streaming down her face. "H-he's dead!"

2

Murder by the Books

SCREECHING SIRENS AND FLASHING LIGHTS descended on
The Happy Bookworm. An ambulance, the sheriff's patrol
car, and several more official vehicles all scattered ever-
whichaways in the spacious driveway. People disembarked,
going on a dead run for the ornate front door of the rejuve-
nated Victorian house. Customers, drawn to the commotion
like metal to a magnet, gravitated to the front window.

At a nod to Rod with a silent message to mind the shop,
Maggie put her arm around the young woman's shaking
shoulders. She led her across the front hall to the kitchen
then shut the door. "What *are* you talking about, Pattysue?
Who's dead?"

Pattysue gulped, took a tissue from the box on the counter, and swiped it across her tear-streaked face. She sat down
at the table, crossed her arms and hunched forward. "It's …
T-Tony, W-Wayne's partner. I'd gone out to pick up our
lunches at the bakery. When I got back, the front door was
wide open. By the first-edition mystery bookshelf up at the
front, you know? Tony … was on the floor. B-blood all over
the back of his coat! I've n-never seen a b-body before!"

Tony Leblanc was Wayne Hardy's business partner as
well as life partner. They owned Hardy's Hardware and

More, a quarter-mile west of the Mercantile on Morrilton Road.

"Wayne was sitting on the floor, crying, with Tony's head in his lap. Harold just stood there. He kept saying, 'I'm sorry. I didn't mean it!' B-but he was holding the gun!"

Maggie blinked in an attempt to sort pronouns, and gave up. "Who was?"

"What?"

"Not what, who?"

"Who was what?"

Maggie felt like she was falling headfirst into the hilarious Abbott and Costello comedy skit: *Who's On First?* She stifled an irreverent giggle. Pattysue was not obtuse, but the young woman seemed to be in shock. Maggie spaced her words out hoping to steer Pattysue back on track. "Who was holding the gun?"

"Oh! The gun." Pattysue blew her nose and sighed. "Wayne."

Larkin Richardson, Maggie's mother, came in, closing the door behind her. "No customers right now. Tea break," she said to Maggie as she turned on the electric teakettle. "Is Harold all right, Pattysue?"

Pattysue nodded. "Yes, Harold's just shook up. Tony Leblanc was shot dead."

"Ah, mercy!" said Larkin.

"Bet he's not too happy about having a real murder beside the classic mystery books. On the one hand, it might be good for business. However, he's not a sensationalist who'd promote Tony's ghost haunting the paranormal mystery stacks," Maggie quipped with a mischievous grin.

Pattysue's smile wavered then her innate good nature won the battle of emotions. "Yes, he is upset ... but I'm scared, Maggie! What if Harold killed him and Wayne took the gun away from him?"

"Harold wouldn't hurt anyone or anything." Larkin set three steaming cups of strong tea on the table.

Hot and strong sweet tea: the panacea for shock, the staple of British cozy mysteries—an effective antidote with or without a rich plummy accent.

"Harold and Wayne didn't get along. Harold's straight, but Wayne and Tony made a pass at him a while back. Tony's own fashion sense was nonexistent, but he was always nice to me when I shopped for curtains and whatnot." Maggie paused to take a careful sip of hot tea. At first, she had been wary of his claims to be a savvy decorator but soon discovered that Tony knew his stuff as far as home décor and designs were concerned. "He's gay and that's his business. Doesn't bother me. It's not enough reason to kill him, at least I would hope humankind is more reasonable than that."

"Pastor Blessington's message last Sunday was on the sixth Commandment. 'No mere mortal has the right to play God in arbitrarily taking another person's life,' was a point he stressed," Larkin said. "He was talking about willful murder, not capital punishment."

Pattysue picked up the steaming mug and took a cautious sip. "Birdie Mandrell's news-vine has it that Wayne and Tony had a horrible spat yesterday, right there in the wallpaper department. Wayne stomped out, looking murderous." She set her mug down. "Maybe Wayne *did* kill him."

3

The Kitty's Meow

Maggie opened the parlor door and went out on the back porch to refill the bird feeder. The porch itself wrapped three sides of the cottage. The upstairs deck was the roof over the back porch. The ceiling was painted light blue to discourage birds and wasps from making nests in the rafters. Somehow, the flying contingent mistook it for sky and left the area alone.

The avian telegraph seemed to be working overtime. She needed to buy another feeder or two, or she'd be refilling this one daily. Just as she moved back, two cardinals landed together on the near edge of the octagonal feeder. Maggie froze. The male picked up a seed and turned to the female. She opened her beak and accepted the love offering. *Aww, how sweet!*

Mrs. Cardinal began rooting through the seeds, tossing the rejects willy-nilly, which fell onto the head of another female cardinal on the ground below the feeder. Miss Cardinal ruffled her feathers, then flew up and made a strafing run for her tormentor.

Drama is everywhere, even in the avian world.

Although wrapped in a heavy cable-knit sweater, she realized it wasn't adequate wear for the chilly thirty-five-degree morning. She had not lived here long enough to re-acclimate to the harsher New England weather. Last night's full moon was known as a Frosty Moon. True to the lunar foreshadowing, the morning was as crisp as a new envelope. A swift breeze off Serenadelle Lake brushed her cheek and sent a shiver down her back. She looked up at heavy clouds, pregnant with the early-warning promise of snow, which excited her. Oklahoma City didn't get much snow, as a rule. When it did, she had rejoiced. Her Okie friends thought she was crazy.

Mist danced over the surface of Serenadelle Lake like diaphanous veils, revealing shy glimpses of the blue-green water. The wind tossed clouds like ghost ships sailing across the cold blue-grey sea of what little sky was visible through the shifting curtain of tree limbs.

She sent up a prayer of thanksgiving. "I am here, really here," she said to the oblivious chipmunk. The scattered sunflower seeds made polka dots on the frost-laden fabric of the dead grass. The little guy paused from stuffing seeds into his chubby cheeks and stared at her. No fear, he went back to his feast.

Chimes emanating from her pocket sent the chipmunk scampering to seek refuge in the pine tree, scolding her with each leap upward. Maggie answered the phone as she returned to the warmth of the parlor. She sat down on the raised hearth of the red brick corner fireplace.

"Good morning, dear. Did I wake you?"

Maggie smiled. The southern-honey voice fell easy on her ears. The woman she'd always known as her aunt was now her mother. Last month, she had learned that her uncle,

Rod Richardson. was in fact her birthfather. The Richardsons had formally adopted the adult Maggie to forestall any problem regarding inheritance, and to bring her without equivocation into the family proper.

"No, Larkin, I was on the back porch having an early-morning chat with a sassy chipmunk," she said.

"Are you enjoying your new home?"

"Very much. I like the short commute to work, too!"

Last month, while the last coat of polyurethane was drying on the floors downstairs, Maggie had set up housekeeping upstairs at the Cottage. In her sitting room, her treasured books were at home on the shelves in alphabetical order by author. Larkin had arranged the books while Maggie organized the office. Evenings, Maggie tackled the master bedroom, the sewing area, and bathroom. She was almost finished. Most of the cardboard boxes were unpacked, broken down, and ready for recycling.

They chatted for several more minutes. Larkin said, "We will come over to the Cottage right after breakfast."

It was early days yet to spot a trend for the shop's busiest times. Until there was some history by which to make plans, Rod and Larkin would be there every day. Pattysue was scheduled to work Thursdays through Saturdays, regardless.

Pattysue Morgan's husband, Robert, was murdered last year. Still a single mom, Pattysue was a hard worker, trying her best to make ends meet. Maggie had helped figure out whodunit, and the two women became friends despite the difference in their ages.

She heard a plaintive high-pitched cry but couldn't place its origin. Tuffy Two-whiskers, her ginger-and-cream kitten, was upstairs, so it wasn't him doing the fussing. She'd left him there, away from the first-week-in-business jitters. The combination door at the top of the stairs was assurance he'd stay put, at least until he was tall enough to figure out how to work the lever handle on the door. The "kitty" doggie door was also latched—from the outside. No cat-Houdini escapes there, either, she hoped.

Maggie was rinsing her cup in the sink when she heard the cry again. This time it seemed to be coming from under the kitchen window. She opened the front door and looked out. A bedraggled and dirty brown cat sat on its scrawny haunches and chirruped. She eased open the combination door and walked slow and easy toward the cat. It stood up in an attitude of flight. Murmuring soft words of assurance, she went down on one knee in front of the shivering feline. It relaxed, approached her and head-bumped her arm.

"Would you like to come in where it's warm? And have some kibble?"

The cat seemed to understand and followed Maggie to the kitchen. She had just put down a small bowl of kibble when Larkin came in from the garage entrance. The cat glanced up at Larkin, tucked its bushy tail around its feet, and buried its face in the bowl.

"Well, I do declare, who's this?" she asked.

"He was on the porch, crying. A stray, by the looks of him, and hungry enough to qualify."

"He looks rather large to be just a common tabby cat."

"Who's your vet? I want to get him checked out first."

"Lisa Beecham-White. She's old Hiram Beecham's granddaughter. Her sister, Rebecca Blackpool, is the Head

Librarian. Lisa's office is part of the Orphan Paws Animal Rescue, on Morrilton Road."

Maggie retrieved the slim phonebook from the kitchen drawer. "Thanks. I'll call her. Just maybe I can get an appointment for sometime today."

The vet said if Maggie could come over right now, she'd see to the cat.

"I'll open and watch the shop if you're not back in time," Larkin said as she held the cat carrier door open.

"Thank you. Now comes the fun part."

Not wishing to be scratched or bitten by a frightened cat, Maggie fell back on what had worked with Tuffy. She wrapped the unhappy feline in a towel before putting him in the carrier.

*****

Maggie liked Lisa Beecham-White on sight and they chatted while the vet ran professional hands along the cat's long sides.

"With his tufted ears, furry toes, rectangular body, triangular head, fluffy tail, and distinctive voice, he's more Maine Coon than tabby. Coons don't reach full growth for another three or four years. Also he's been de-clawed on front and neutered." Lisa said. "He will be an armful when he's grown."

"He already is," Maggie replied.

"You just wait!" Lisa laughed. "This is my vet assistant, Wanda Trask. Her brother, Wayne, owns Hardy's Hardware."

"Pleased to meet you, Wanda. Wanda and Wayne, you're

11

not twins, are you?" Maggie asked.

"Heavens, no." Wanda smiled as she tested the water running in a tall, deep tub. "My parents' names are Wilber and Wilhamena Hardy. Mother went overboard on 'W' names. There's Wayne, myself, Walter, Wilma, and Waldo is the baby of the family." She donned a plastic poncho and long heavy rubber gloves. "*My* kids do *not* have 'W' names." She lifted the cat off the table, held his back legs together and plunked him into the tub.

Maggie stayed back to keep from getting drenched by any backwash. Wanda seemed to have a way with the art of cat washing. The cat talked to Wanda, though to Maggie's cat-attuned ear, it did not sound much like compliments he was tossing her way.

A little over an hour later, Maggie returned to the Cottage. "Lisa gave the cat his shots and a clean bill of health. Wanda gave him a bath. He didn't mind that as much as when she turned the warm-air-dryer on."

"Poor baby. The noise would scare him more than the breeze, I would think," Larkin said.

"Lisa agreed that he was abandoned, discarded like he was so much garbage. I don't need to tell you what name she called *those* people! He looks full-grown, but he isn't. He's about nine months old now. Neutered, and de-clawed on front."

"Someone took care of him, once upon a time, at least." Larkin peeked in the carrier. "Interesting spot of rust-colored fur on his nose. Looks like a thumbprint."

"Quite true. Then I'll call him Rusty Thumbkin."

"That's a cute name. I hope Tuffy will get along with

12

him," Larkin said as she flipped the switch to turn on the "Open" sign.

"We are about to find out." Maggie lugged the carrier upstairs. "You're no lightweight already, Rusty, I hope you know."

"Ruffow!" Rusty agreed.

Tuffy was perched on the sitting room windowsill watching squirrels scampering in the tree limbs when Maggie came in with the carrier. He stood up with his ears perked forward, jumped down, and sniffed the carrier. He greeted the newcomer, *"Mee-row!"*

Rusty mewed and chirped. With no snarls or growls forthcoming from either feline, she opened the hatch. Rusty popped up and jumped out. Within a few minutes, after a thorough sniffing of each other fore and aft, the cats began playing a rough and tumble game of keep-away. Both were males and almost the same age, but Tuffy was much smaller. Even so, in those first moments, somehow Tuffy established himself as Alpha cat. He seemed happy to have a playmate here since his fur buddies, Siam and Sheba, lived at Eagles' Rest.

She snatched Rusty in mid-run and took him in the bathroom. She showed him the litter box and food bowl. Cats have a sophisticated sense of smell, so Rusty could have found these things on his own with no help from her. However, it was a ritual she did with every cat that had ever owned her.

Satisfied that all was well above stairs, Maggie went down to start the second day of business.

She wondered who had killed Tony Leblanc. Just as sure

as apples make applesauce, Maggie knew that Harold did not kill Tony. The gentle bookseller sold murder mysteries but did not hold with murder itself.

4

Speaking of Widows

Right after lunch, Maggie went upstairs to check on the cats. They were both on the bed with their front paws tucked under them, wearing angelic expressions on their sweet furry faces. However, a suspicious scattering of white tissue, like crumbs along a trail, leading from the bathroom told another story. A roll of toilet tissue had been subdued into submission and duly dispatched, with pieces of tissue still floating on the air current like funky bridal confetti.

"What mischief have you two been up to?" she scolded, although it was obvious.

Two pairs of eye-blinks followed by massive yawns in chorus seemed to say, "Who, *moi?*"

She ran the hand sweeper to get up most of the little white bits. Wondering how to best thwart a repeat performance, she remembered several baskets stashed in the far corner of her sewing closet. Sure enough, she found a flat-backed white wicker basket that might work, and a short over-door J-hook. Both cats followed her into the bathroom, watching her with interest. There was a towel rod quite high up on the wall beside the toilet. She hung the top hook over the bar, hung the basket on the J-hook, and put in a new roll of tissue. "That ought to fix your little furry wagons."

Sherrill M. Lewis

Rusty sprang up on the toilet seat. He stretched a paw out for the basket. It swung away when he touched it. Over-reaching on his unsteady narrow perch and losing his balance, he nearly dunked himself. Maggie laughed at his near mishap. Rusty shook the water off his hind paw then jumped down to chase Tuffy.

When she arrived back downstairs, she found Elda Carmichael, Baysinger Cove's Mayor, wandering around the shop. "Looks like you're pretty busy for being open only a day."

"Yes, and I'm glad for it. What can I do for you?"

Elda was also a talented crazy quilter. A recent widow in her early sixties, she filled her days with politicking, volunteering for worthy causes, town business, and staying active. At the moment, however, she had mayoral business on her agenda. "Specifically, the ribbon-cutting for your Grand Opening that I mentioned last month. How about Saturday, the twenty-second?"

Maggie looked at the calendar hanging on the wall beside the cash desk. *Eight days away and right before Thanksgiving week. Good timing.* "That's fine." *Eight days away. Yikes!*

"Hot cider and cookies for the festivities? Does ten o'clock suit you?"

Maggie agreed and wrote it on the calendar.

"I'd love to shop now, but I've got to get this up to the *Baywater County Chronicle* within the next hour. We want a big splash in next Friday's paper. I'll get it up on the town's website, too."

Eight days. "I'll take care of the goodies and hot cider."

Maggie wrote a detailed note on a small, lined sticky-note pad, pulled off the sheet and stuck it on the calendar for tomorrow. *Order cookies from Sweet Things, pastries from Kasha's, and gallons of cider from the Mercantile.*

"Any grand opening day specials?" Elda interrupted Maggie's concentration.

Maggie tapped her bottom lip with the pen. "The first fifteen paying customers with at least a twenty-five dollar purchase will receive a ten-dollar gift certificate. And there will be discounts on classes for all fifty-dollar and hundred-dollar purchases made that day."

"That's very generous. Thank you. Now, about joining the Chamber of Commerce—"

Something Maggie had no desire to join, in neither the near nor distant future, so she stalled, interrupting Elda's soliloquy. "Don't you need to head to the newspaper office? The deadline is coming up."

Elda glanced at her watch. "By golly, you're right." She tucked her cherry-red, fuzzy scarf inside her full-length, blue wool coat as she headed for the door. "I've got to get this typed up PDQ! See you later."

A woman laid a crazy quilt block down on the cutting table. "My name is Artesia Lovington. So, what do you think?" she asked, patting the block.

The two women in line behind Artesia crowded forward and made appreciative noises as they examined her exquisite work. "I hope to be that good someday," one said in a wistful voice.

The other one nodded agreement. "Me, too. Someday."

Maggie surveyed the complex thread embroidery stitches

and the intricate silk ribbon work. "It's beautiful, Miss Artesia. You certainly know what you're doing."

"I've been crazy quilting all my life. My mother taught me. Oh, mercy, you're waiting for me and there are people behind me!"

"What pretties did you find this time, Miss Artesia?" Maggie asked.

"Just these. Missed them before." Artesia laid a stack of lace appliqués and several packages of exquisite buttons on the counter. "Has Sheriff Bainbridge arrested anyone yet?"

"Not that I'm aware of, he hasn't. The murder only happened yesterday, for pity sakes," Maggie answered as she totaled Artesia's purchases. "He's good, but give him a break."

"Shouldn't be *that* difficult," Artesia sniffed. "Wayne was found with Tony's blood all over his clothes and the gun in his hand. How much detecting should *that* take?"

*****

Maggie stood in the parlor near the CD player choosing several stacks of soft easy-listening instrumentals, and putting away the previous ones before chaos took over. Pattysue was sitting at the kitchen table having lunch with her mother-in-law. It was the right-after-lunch lull, and the Cottage was quiet, except for their loud argument.

"Charlee, I have every right to date whoever I want to. It's my life, not yours. Cooper Larradeau loves Kaleen and she loves him back."

"But your sister Carrie murdered my baby boy. I won't

have you marrying the husband of his murderer. Cooper is your *brother*-in-law." The multi-strand red Austrian crystal necklace swinging side-to-side accentuated the melodrama.

It was obvious from her rigid posture that Pattysue was holding onto her temper with both hands. "It's not *incest,* for heaven's sake, Charlee. You know darn well that Cooper divorced Carrie before she even went to trial. And you refuse to see that your *precious baby boy* was a womanizer, a liar, a drunkard, and a batterer." Pattysue set her drink down so hard that Maggie feared for the life expectancy of the glass. "And, I will marry who I want to. I don't care if you approve or not."

"Well!" Charlotte huffed, tossed her head, and wiped her mouth. Her necklace gave a dangerous lurch toward starboard then went leeward. A renegade beam of sunlight bounced off her matching bracelet, scattering prisms of color across the table. "You should at least honor the *memory* of your daughter's father. It's still too soon for you to marry again anyway."

Maggie's thoughts ran to the customs of the nineteenth century. For the first year, only the dullest black dresses were worn with no ornamentation. Hats were not allowed; instead the widow wore cloth bonnets, just as dull. The second year, black lace cuffs and collars adorned the dull black for perhaps six months. Entering the third year of mourning, rich black, grey, violet or white relieved the somber hues of the first eighteen months. Almost three years of widowhood!

She was glad that the twenty-first-century women had gained a more realistic perspective on the etiquette of widowhood. In the early 1970s, she herself was widowed, and she'd never remarried. Not that she hadn't had several long-term romances. Nonetheless, no one was, well, the *right* one. CJ Dubois was her high-school sweetheart. Now the mature man was the current prime candidate—if she'd just give over and agree to marry the tall Texan-returned-Yankee.

Whatcha gonna do, Maggie Storm Blue? In the late 1960s, when she was first married, her handsome husband, well-known songwriter and guitarist, Kiernan Irish Blue, had written a love song for her. He came home one week from the end of his second tour of Vietnam with a Purple Heart and a flag-draped casket. The catchy tag line often came to mind whenever she was discouraged, in a dilemma, or disheartened. Other than that, she did not bring Kiernan himself to mind very often any more. When she did, no love, no hurt, no feeling whatsoever, attended the passing thought. Time passages. Maggie left the past in the past where it belonged. Today and tomorrow mattered.

"Being married to Robert Morgan is a memory I'd just as soon forget, Charlee. Are you saying I should be a widow *forever*?" Pattysue took a spoonful of peanuts out of the covered candy dish and scattered them on her plate.

"Of course not. What about that nice doctor? That Roy Grayson, he's got a promising future in medicine. He'll make good money, too. But don't you neglect my little Kaleen, not for one minute, Pattysue. I raised my Robert, God rest his precious soul. She's all I have left of my poor baby." The necklace entered the swing of things again before settling down against Charlotte's short neck.

Maggie slipped six discs on the CD turntable and pushed the button for random play.

The *Baywater County Chronicle* was on the kitchen table, where Rod had left it earlier, folded so that the story of the murder at the bookstore was uppermost.

Charlotte glanced at it and gasped. "W-what's this? 'Murder in the Mystery Stack'?"

"Didn't you know? Wayne found him."

"No! It can't be ... " She put her hand over her heart. A second too late, she added, "Oh, that's too bad." She ran a manicured nail down the first paragraph. "What was he doing in there?"

"Buying books, probably. You buy books there, but you don't like Harold."

"Um, oh, that's right. Then ... who's Wayne?"

"Wayne Hardy and Tony Leblanc own Hardy's Hardware. Tony was also Wayne's life partner."

"Oh. *Those* two." Charlotte wrinkled her nose like she'd just stepped in something nasty. "Well, that's why he was in the bookstore. Three of a—"

"Don't you dare say it, Charlee!" Pattysue pushed the dish of peanuts toward her mother-in-law.

"I can't eat peanuts!" Charlotte exclaimed. "I'm allergic."

"Oh, sorry. I didn't know."

She stood up and put on her coat. "I'm going to Waterville this afternoon. I'll get my sweet little Kaleen a new dress."

"Don't bother, Charlee. She doesn't need anything. Stop spoiling her." Pattysue glanced at her watch and dismissed her mother-in-law with a curt goodbye. She stood up and gathered the detritus of their lunches. "I have to get back to

21

work now. Here're your gloves."

Maggie had just finished putting away the CDs from yesterday's play set when the front door opened. Harold Tottenbaum poked his head around the kitchen door. "Maggie? You busy?"

"Be right there, my friend."

Charlotte looked at Harold and went slack-jawed. Muttering under her breath, she shrugged into her coat, snatched the gloves from her daughter-in-law, and stalked out the front door.

Pattysue told Maggie as they went into the shop, "Not sure what she was mumbling about. Sometimes I think she's going senile. Besides her so-called peanut allergy, which this is the first I heard of it, she has another incurable affliction: a severely over-inflated ego."

"You are so funny, Pattysue, whether you mean to be or not!" Both women dissolved into a giggle fit.

"Here are the books you ordered," Harold said as Maggie came up for air and joined him. "And I want the grand tour, if you're simply not too busy." He glanced around and his smile spread from one pudgy cheek to the other. "Wow! This is fabulous."

Maggie wrote him a check for the three new Anne Perry books he had brought with him. They talked shop for about thirty minutes before Harold took himself back across the street to his own store.

*****

At three-thirty, Maggie watched the big yellow school

22

bus stop at the entrance to Cranberry Lane. Kaleen hopped down the steps one at a time then waved to the bus driver. He waited until she opened the Cottage door before pulling back onto the street.

Kaleen bounced into the kitchen, shrugged off her hot pink backpack and set it on a chair.

"Roy's coming over to our house tonight. He's bringing pizza. Sound good?" Pattysue shucked Kaleen out of her bulky outerwear and planted a kiss on her daughter's weather-reddened cheek.

"Pizza? Yay! I like Roy, even when he doesn't bring pizza. Are we going to marry him, Mama?"

"He hasn't asked us."

"Oh, he will!"

Pattysue laughed and gave her daughter a quick hug before going across to the shop to help the customers who had just come in.

Maggie was only a holler away if Pattysue needed help, so she joined the happy little girl at the kitchen table. Kaleen had oatmeal-raisin cookies with milk, and Maggie had hot tea with hers. They discussed Kaleen's adventures at school until the child changed subjects. "Mama works for you. I want a job, too."

Maggie wasn't sure about having an employee the height of the front doorknob, not to mention weeding through the morass of child-labor laws. "Why do you want a job?"

"To make some money." She gave Maggie a milk-mustache grin. "You're silly!"

"Why do you want to make money?"

"To put in my piggy bank."

Dumb question!

"What will you do when your piggy bank is full?"

"Buy Mommy a new house."

"That's an admirable goal."

"I think so." Kaleen scrunched her pert little face in concentration. "Um, what's admir-blue mean?"

"Admirable means it's splendid, worthy, or good. You have a splendid goal."

"You're an admir … admirable cook." Kaleen ate her cookie then smiled. "I still need a job."

"Thank you." Maggie finished her own cookie. "Let me think on that a while. I'll get back to you later, okay?"

"Okay. May I have some more milk?"

5

Masks and Masquerades

"ARE YOU GOING TO THE MASQUERADE BALL tonight?" Maggie's customer asked her.

The Autumn Ball was one of two annual fundraisers for the Baywater County Arts Council. Proceeds helped pay for the upkeep of the Art Depot and bring in famous artists for art demonstrations and programs. The theme changed from year to year.

In the spring, they hosted a variety of other events, such as a progressive gourmet dinner, an Old West fashion show complete with a chow wagon, an art auction, or whatever their creative minds could conceive. Birdie's news-vine was all a-flutter with the news that the Council members were planning a pirate ship adventure for next year.

"No. I didn't find out about it in time." Maggie glanced at the name on the credit card to refresh her memory before handing it back to the woman. "Who are you going as, Lucy, an author's best-known character or a movie character?"

"Lucille Ball!" The former brunette giggled and patted her flaming red curls.

Her friend looked over the top of her granny glasses. "That color's good on you. I think you should keep it."

"Maybe I will. Who did you finally decide to go as,

Mary?"

"I love *The Ghost and Mrs. Muir*. I settled on her. My husband's going as the ghost. Can you imagine him as a ghost?"

"At his size, no I can't!" Lucy replied.

"I thought about going as Tamar Meyer's Penn-Dutch gal Madeline Yoder," their companion said as she put her shopping basket on the checkout counter.

"You'd need to work on the sass and alliteration to pull that one off, Coretta," Mary advised.

"Too much effort and no time to do it in." Coretta looked perplexed then she brightened. "I know! Laurel Darling Roethke. Don't you just love Carolyn Hart's character? I've read every book in the Death on Demand series. I think I can be sexy sweet, and oh-so-precious!"

"You've certainly got that down in spades," Lucy sputtered before laughing outright at the attitude and sultry walk her friend struck as she sashayed around.

Quiet until now, Tina piped up, "I'm Miss Marple, and I have the knitting to go with it!" She held up a calico tote bag and pulled out a half-completed red fuzzy scarf.

If I were to choose, it would be Patricia Wentworth's Miss Silver, without the knitting, or maybe ... Maggie's thoughts were interrupted by the front door slamming open, bouncing as it hit the wall.

The Lone Ranger took a theatrical stance in the middle of the shop's wide doorway. Today's incarnation was a man of average height, but too chunky for the role. He stood with his chino-clad legs spread apart in a perfect imitation of the Ranger's classic quick-draw stance—except for the AK-15 assault rifle he raised from his hip.

The four women froze in horror as he swung the gun in a sweeping arc back and forth several times. He clicked the trigger.

"Rat-a-tat-tat!"

Dead silence.

"Ha-ha! Gotcha!" As he lowered the rifle, his cold and calculating dark brown eyes behind the black mask assessed Maggie for a long minute. His beard was more white than brown. The man spewed out a polluted stream of vitriolic words before he spun around and limped toward the door.

His world must be minuscule if the limits of his language define the limits of his world. For pity's sake! The man just pulled an assault weapon on us, and I'm thinking about his word choices? Sheesh! I should be a blithering idiot or something!

For what seemed like several centuries, the silence following the man's exit was absolute. Then the spell broke, and the women all started talking at once.

"Did you know who that was?" Maggie asked, wading through the chatter.

"I was too busy looking at the gun to see the man holding it," Mary replied with a violent shudder.

"I liked to have wet my pants," Lucy said, her ashen face a stark contrast to her red curls. "Weren't you scared, Maggie?"

Coretta gulped. "H-he's not a regular customer, is he?" She sank down on a chair near the cutting table beside Tina.

Tina hadn't said a word and was staring at nothing. Her face changed color, and she slid to the floor in a jumble of red wool yarn.

Whatcha gonna do, Maggie Storm Blue?

Call the sheriff, of course! But I heartily wish you'd get out of my head already!

6

Reporter and Reports

"**HI, MS. BLUE!** I'm Nellwyn Westron, reporter for the 'Baysinger Cove Town Crier' section of the *Baywater County Chronicle*." At first glance, her spiked purple and orange hair caused Maggie's eyebrows to rise a quarter inch, until the girl smiled. "Please call me Nell."

"Please call me Maggie, and come on in."

They settled at the kitchen table. "Are you any relation to John Westron?" She referred to the Clipper Ship Band's talented lead singer at the Rusty Anchor.

"Yeah, he's my father. I'm the youngest of four girls. The only one who isn't musically inclined, but Dad's finally accepted it since I have my own byline now. He was pleased, too, when I wrote the words for one of their most popular songs." The happy pride of this major accomplishment in her all-musical-but-one family showed all over the young woman's face.

A few minutes later the photographer arrived. Skin leathery from too many years in the sun, he squinted as he slid yellow-mirrored sunglasses up on his head. The camera hugged his neck as if he were born wearing it. With long gray hair pulled back in a low ponytail and his full beard the same shade of gray, he resembled an old hippie out of time but not out of place. Unpretentious—however, a man not to be dismissed as *just* a photographer.

Maggie recognized his name. Mike Richaud was one of the best art photographers on the eastern seaboard. His photographs were on display at Art at the Depot and in art galleries nationwide. When she was here for a two-week vacation last Christmas, she had gone with Larkin to the Depot where she saw Mike's work for the first time. She loved the one with dozens of butterflies taking flight, and told him so. His answering shy smile transformed his face, and she liked him all the more for his humble heart.

"I'm curious why you, a well-known photographer, are taking pictures for a small-town newspaper?" Maggie asked as he stepped back to get a full shot of her crazy quilt.

"Their regular guy's on his honeymoon. I'm filling in. Giving a little back to the county I was born in." He turned to the reporter. "Anything else you need, Nell?"

After Mike finished taking pictures and took his leave, Nell asked, "So, like, what are your plans for teaching?"

"In late January, depending on the weather, of course, classes will start up. All the way from beginner to advanced, both beading and all aspects of crazy quilting. Right now, I am asking each of my customers to fill out a questionnaire so I can structure classes around the need."

Last week, right after Nell called to make an appointment, Maggie sat down at her computer and wrote the full story. She handed the document to the reporter. "In case you have questions or need clarification and you're on deadline," she explained. "Not to imply that you are unable to write an accurate story, of course." Past experience had taught Maggie well.

"No offense taken. What was that scene with the Lone Ranger look-alike yesterday?" Nell asked, flipping her notebook over for a clean page.

Birdie's news-vine is alive and thriving. Gossip to her is as natural as breathing. "Somebody wanting to show off his costume for the Ball, I guess. No harm done, other than scaring the be-whalers out of us." Maggie had dismissed the man's jaded invectives as the trash they were. She wondered about the calculating look he gave her before limping out, but kept her thoughts to herself.

Caught mid-daydream, she reined in her truant wits to attend to Nell's comment and only caught the tail end.

"The scuttlebutt, according to Birdie anyway, says it was a real gun," Nell was saying, giving Maggie a quizzical look.

"It sure looked like one. Not that I would really know the difference. Thankfully there was no ammo in it." Maggie shivered with the memory that was too fresh in her head. The only guns she'd ever handled were her grandfather's single-shot bolt-action .22 caliber rifle, and *his* father's 1896 Iver Johnson revolver. It was a small handgun with an owl carved in the ornate handle. *They should still be in one or the other of the two boxes I haven't unpacked since forever.*

They moved to the hallway where the sign Joe Greylock had created for her rested on an easel at the foot of the stairs. "Where'd you come up with the name?"

"I'm just crazy about butterflies. Second Corinthians five-seventeen. Like the butterfly emerges from its ugly case, through Christ I am also a new creation."

"Wow, that's awesome. Butterflies are your logo, so why

didn't you name your company 'Butterfly Crazy'?"

Maggie laughed. "The Spanish word is *mariposa,* which is prettier than the French *papillion*." She led Nell over to the cutting table. The crazy quilt was hanging on the wall behind the L of the cutting table and cash desk, well out of reach of sticky fingers and harmful sunlight. "This was the inspiration for the name of my shop. It's called *Joyfully Fritillary Crazy*. There are well over a hundred butterflies on the front, of one kind or another." She lifted a corner to show Nell the riotous butterfly fabric backing. "But I refuse to count the ones on the back!"

"I don't blame you! It's, like, simply gorgeous. I hope Mike got a good picture of that."

"He certainly did. Now over here we have ..."

Maggie led Nell around the shop. Pedestals of varying heights grouped together showcased seasonal-themed items. The first set was all about autumn and Thanksgiving with orange, russet, gold, and brown trims, ribbons, and buttons arranged in wicker baskets. Near it, a round table held items related to Christmas and the December holidays showcased in large glass dishes, antique punchbowls, and silver-wire baskets.

"When we move out Thanksgiving items and bring Christmas forward, we'll showcase January's colors: blue, white and silver." Returning to the front, Maggie introduced the young reporter to Larkin.

"It's cool how you've arranged the beads. Sort of like unfolding the color wheel." Nell turned full circle, her eyes wide. "Wow, you've got, like, everything here!"

"Almost," Larkin agreed. "Would you be interested in

taking any classes?"

"I might be." Nell checked her phone. "Gotta run, but I'll be back when you've got the classes figured out. Let me know, and I'll post it on the community calendar page. Thanks for talking to me today."

"You are most welcome, and thank you, too." After Nell departed Maggie said to Larkin, "Did you hear that? With all Nell seems willing to do for us, I'd best think about purchasing ad space."

"That would only be fair. Any news about Tony's murderer, though?" Larkin asked. "Does Walker have a suspect in mind?"

"Haven't heard anything." She glanced out the front window. A patrol car pulled in the driveway and parked in front of the garage. "Speaking of the sheriff, I'd better put the coffee on. He just drove up, and we can ask him."

Maggie poured fresh coffee into a stout ceramic mug and set it on the kitchen table in front of her lawman friend, along with napkins and a plate heaped with white chocolate coconut cookies. "How's the investigation going?"

"Slow. At first it looked really bad for Wayne Hardy." Sheriff Walker Bainbridge reached for a cookie and took a big bite.

"How so?" Maggie couldn't resist, even if it was her own baking, so she also took a cookie.

"He kept saying he was sorry, which sure didn't sound good. Turns out he was referring to the screaming argument they'd had at the store the other day." He reached for two cookies this time. "These are wicked good."

"Thanks. It's one of my favorite recipes."

"When do you have time to bake?" He swallowed coffee to wash down the third cookie.

"First thing in the morning, or at night, if it's quiet here. I enjoy Stella's cookies and Kasha's goodies, and I patronize them frequently. But the smell of fresh-baked cookies helps sweeten most customers' attitudes, too."

Back on subject, she said, "I heard Wayne was found holding the gun. That sounds awfully incriminating."

"The shooter wore gloves. There were no fingerprints other than Wayne's, everywhere except on the trigger. There was a piece of red fuzzy lint caught in the trigger. I sent it to the lab. May be nothing, but every bit tells a story."

"I remember you telling me that before. Like pieces of a puzzle." Maggie refilled their mugs.

"Come to find out, Wayne's terrified of guns. Don't know why he even picked it up."

"Unconscious reaction, I suppose. Moving the weapon away from the body negates the horror, disassociating the weapon from the deadly result? That's one for the psychiatrists. Not me."

She reached for another cookie, silently thanking the genetic pool for giving her a metabolism that kept her thin regardless of what she ate. "One of my customers thought it was a car backfiring. Maybe it was old Hiram's cranky jalopy. Of course, I flashbacked to that long-ago bank robbery in Tucson." Had she not been on break at the time the robbers came in, she would have died along with the young bank teller.

"Naturally you would. Did you see anything?"

Maggie thought back to the first day of business. "I heard

34

the noise and glanced out the window. The bookstore's front door was wide open, which is probably why I heard anything at all. A few seconds later, someone in a dark coat came out in a big hurry and didn't close the door. A delivery truck went by just then and blocked everything, and then a customer distracted me. We were swamped that first day." The door chime rang again. "Still are, I am pleased to say." She slid the remaining cookies into a plastic bag and handed it to the happy lawman.

"I am glad for you, too, Maggie. You deserve success. Thanks for the coffee, and the cookies. I'd better go. Let me know if you hear anything."

"I will. Please save at least a few of the cookies for Abigail." His wife owned Snippets, the wonderful quilt store about a half-mile north on Franklin Road.

"If I have to," he winked. "Got to run by the store anyway. Later!"

In October, on her second voyage on the stormy sea of sleuthing, the sheriff had intimated that he'd like to have her on his staff. She had demurred, not wanting to burn bridges, but she had to focus on getting her shop up and running. They had compromised, and Maggie agreed to be an occasional consultant. Without putting too fine of a point on it, she would keep her ears and eyes open. So far, regarding this murder, she hadn't seen or heard anything useful.

7

Small Stuff

KALEEN MORGAN WAS SITTING at the kitchen table with a pencil and paper when Maggie came in to get a drink of water. Her little face was scrunched up in concentration.

"Whatcha doin', Kaleen?"

"Playing a numbers game," the precocious five-year-old answered. "Want to play?"

It was nearing closing time, and there was only one customer in the shop. Pattysue was taking care of her, so Maggie sat down next to Kaleen. "Sure. What do I do first?"

"Pick any number from one to nine and write it down." Kaleen tore a fresh sheet off her pad then handed it and a pencil to Maggie.

Maggie said and wrote, "Five."

"Now multiply it by three and add three."

"Fifteen plus three equals eighteen."

"Okay, now multiply that by three." Kaleen slid out of her chair to stand beside Maggie.

"It's fifty-four," Maggie said. "Now what?"

"Add the five and four together. You get nine!"

"Quite true. What's so special about that?"

"Use any number and nine is always the final answer! Isn't that fun?"

"It certainly is." Maggie hugged the little girl. "You are a very smart young lady." *Incredibly smart—she'll give her teachers a run for their money, if she hasn't already!* Remembering one of her own grade school teachers, way back when, she amended the aphorism: *Apoplectic fit!*

"Where did you learn this trick?"

She climbed back up into her chair. "Bampaw teaches me number games. That's fun! But I like it better when Bammaw reads to me. She really likes it when I read to her."

"What book are you reading now?"

"*Stuart Little,* it's my favorite." She dug around in her pink backpack until she pulled out a book. "We're reading this one next. *The Magical Ms. Plum,* that sounds fun!"

Pattysue came in and stood beside Kaleen. Kaleen excused herself then scooted out of her chair and headed toward the bathroom.

Stuart Little by E.B. White and *The Magical Ms. Plum* by Bonny Becker were both third-grade level books. "Kaleen's reading at that level already?" Maggie asked Pattysue.

"She knows most of the words, and her comprehension is high. My family and I are all readers. We prefer entertainment through fiction without the adrenalin rushes of mind-numbing TV fare. Charlee helped clean out Bob's things, and I sent our small portable TV with her. We stay busy enough without a TV. We don't miss it, either."

Kaleen skipped her way back to the kitchen. Pattysue held out her coat. "Time to go, Kaleen. We're going to Bampaw and Bammaw's house for dinner tonight. How's that sound?"

After Kaleen finished her happy dance so her mother

could get the child's coat on, Maggie asked, "These are your parents?"

"Yes. Henry and Audra Davidsby. They love her to pieces and teach her things beyond her years, which she soaks up like water to a sponge." She pulled up the hood on her daughter's coat. "You read to me sometimes, too, don't you, Kalie-girl?" Kaleen nodded, making it hard for her mother to tie a bow under the pert little chin. "Hold still, wiggle worm!"

After she closed the shop, Maggie toyed with using double digits as the beginning number. At the last step, she ended up with a three-digit answer. However, adding those final digits together, she still came up with nine. 45x3 = 135, +3 = 138. 138 x 3 = 414. 4+1+4 = 9.

Ever curious, she tried triple and quadruple digits to start, always with the same result.

She recalled a classmate who was a whiz with numbers. Steve Longmaster once told her that nine was magical as well as meaning transportation. Where he came up with that theory was anybody's guess. In Kaleen's game, it always brought the final answer to be nine. *Interesting.*

Pythagoras, the father of modern numerology, had a different, very occult, stance on numbers, and would disagree with her math major friend. This game was fascinating, but Maggie's happy camp was with words.

8

Respite

"COME ON, MAGGIE. We should celebrate the success of your first week in business." CJ reached up and brushed a lock of silver-laced black hair behind her ear. "I made reservations at the Pennyroyal. It'll do you good."

"As much as I'd love to go dancing, I probably wouldn't last out one set. A quiet dinner with you sounds wonderful."

CJ's mustache was grown out now, though the dark brown was mixed with streaks of gray.

"You look like Marty Robbins," she said, kissing him.

"Can't sing like him. Wish I could." He returned her kiss with double interest.

"Don't be modest. You don't set the dogs a-howling like my step-father used to do."

CJ laughed. "That reminds me of a saying down home. If there's a circle around the moon and your dog howls at it, sure as shootin', a storm and company are coming in at the same time."

"Quite true. Often the two are synonymous, or better yet, synchronistic," she said, remembering the contentious and hateful natures of her erstwhile sisters. When they came visiting it *was* stormy weather. Beryl, Amber, and Ruby were now in prison and would be for a very long time.

CJ glanced at his watch. "It's getting on for six, *querida*. We need to leave soon."

Business had been very good all week, and today exceeded her wildest expectations. If these first four days were any indication of the activity of days to come, she'd need to hire more help. Though she would rather stay home tonight, the old adage of all work and no play was true. She also knew the pitfalls of ignoring her best beau. As devoted as CJ was to her, she loved and respected him enough that she had no wish to try his patience. Everyone has a breaking point.

CJ waited in her sitting room while she changed out of jeans in favor of a long dark blue silk-denim skirt. The Pennyroyal expected far nicer dress than ratty jeans and a beer-logo t-shirt, but did not lean to tux and gown, unless one wished to dress that way.

Maggie stood in the doorway fussing with a dangle earring that wanted to twist. "Interesting that you chose that chair."

That chair. Rusty was sitting in CJ's lap while Tuffy sat on top of the back cushion in Grandfather's Morris chair. Maggie loved the antique chair. It was made of solid oak with claw feet and growling lion's head arms. In the past, how men reacted to that chair spoke volumes. Over time, she had discovered a direct correlation between their opinion of the chair and the success, or failure, of the budding relationship. Many years ago, she had replaced the decrepit horse-hair-filled cracked leather cushions with upholstery-covered, button-tufted, batting-wrapped foam cushions.

"It's comfortable." He reached up to swat Tuffy's tail out of his face. "How are the cats getting along?"

Rusty hopped down.

"Best friends now, it seems. They are young and about the same age, which helps."

Tuffy leaped off the back of the chair and joined Rusty, who was curling up in a tight ball on the loveseat.

*****

Once they were seated in one of the Pennyroyal's dining alcoves and had placed their orders, CJ took her delicate hand in his large one. Dark came early this time of year so they could not see the majestic Atlantic Ocean beyond the wall of windows, but they could hear her soundings as the breakers crashed with a mighty roar against the granite cliff.

"Where'd you learn to dance?" CJ asked after the waiter delivered their drinks.

"It's a two-part story. First, when I was eleven, I learned ballroom dancing: waltz, foxtrot, and cha-cha. It must have been part of the school curriculum since I don't remember Grandfather taking me to special dance lessons."

CJ put down his wine glass. "What's the second part? Country?"

"Yes." Maggie smiled with the recollection. "Friends invited me to meet them at a bar downtown where a favorite local band was playing. I'd never been there before and wasn't sure what to wear. I settled on a silk blouse, pressed jeans, and heels, and I was way over-dressed for that crowd."

"Must have been a honky-tonk, then."

"It was. A wood banister fenced off the dance floor from the seating area. Our table was right next to the banister and my chair was backed up against the railing. A cowboy tapped me on the shoulder and asked me to dance. I told him I was trapped, obviously. Before I could say boy howdy, he'd picked me up and hoisted me over the rail onto the dance floor. When I told him I didn't know the dance, he laughed. 'Little darlin', I'll teach you,' he told me. Before that song was over I had the basics of a two-step down. When the band finished their set, I had learned most of the fancy moves and turns."

"I'm glad you stuck with it. And that you are *my* dance partner now."

"So am I. We do make a good team."

They abandoned conversation to attend to the sumptuous feast the waiter set before them.

"It's been a super busy week for you, *querida*." CJ finished his baked potato.

"Quite. It's early days yet to know how well the business will do, but so far, so good. Meanwhile, I'm wondering who killed Tony, and why anyone would want to murder him. Right this minute though, it feels good to sit and not think," Maggie said after swallowing the last bit of the succulent baked scallops. "Though with Thanksgiving a bare ten days away, I'd best be thinking about *that* very soon. What are your plans?"

CJ wiped his mouth and laid his napkin across his plate. "Most years, since Ann died, Michaela and Chase swap Thanksgiving holidays. We take turns, either going to Seattle to be with Michaela, or in Texas with Chase at the Rockin' Diamond D Ranch."

"This year?"

"It's Michaela's turn."

"Oh." Maggie tried to not show her disappointment, but she never was a good poker player.

"Don't fret, *querida*." He patted her hand. "It's your first holiday with your new-found family. I want to be here with you."

"Oh, CJ, thank you." She leaned over to kiss him. "I would understand, sweetheart, but I would have missed you."

"Unless you came with me."

"This year especially, being here with my mother and father means the world to me." She paused, reflecting on his last comment. "What did you mean by 'come with you'?"

"Just what I said. Fly with me to visit the kids."

"Why not invite them to come here? Maybe every third year?"

"That's a thought."

"Perhaps next year I'll go with you to Texas so I can meet them on common ground before they descend on us here in unfamiliar territory. They may not even like me."

"Chase is forty-four and Michaela is forty-two. They are adults. You'll do fine, Maggie."

"I hope so," she replied.

In October, remodeling the cottage to function as a shop as well as her domicile, and putting together a business plan were her first priorities—after ferreting out the half-dozen people who had escalated mischief and mayhem to malevolency and murder. Facing down her three diabolical sisters, she slew the metaphorical dragon. On the heels of learning that her beloved uncle was her biological father, she was legally adopted into the Richardson family. That CJ was planning future holidays with her solidified Maggie's standing in that relationship.

During that malicious onslaught she hadn't gotten much rest. It had been scary yet exciting to bring the evil-deed-doers to justice. Adrenalin rushes could be addictive, she realized. She far preferred solving mysteries vicariously with her favorite cozy-mystery authors than chasing real desperadoes.

9

A Rose Unnamed

MAGGIE WAS STANDING IN THE PARLOR looking out at Serenadelle Lake when she heard the front door open. CJ came in, and they met in the kitchen.

"Come, look at this." He beckoned her to the front porch.

She slipped on a long black wool cape and followed him out to the front porch. "What?"

"This." He pointed to her left.

She had placed an old-fashioned student desk, a housewarming gift from Chad and Autumn Taylor, near the front door. On top of the desk was a heavy black tin box painted with red roses, daisies, and a colorful butterfly for decoration. Words in ornate script on the lid advised: "Leave a note." Beside the box lay a rose so dark red it appeared black. Wrapped in the black satin ribbon along with the rose were two sticks of black licorice-twist candy fastened in an X configuration.

This one stumped her. While CJ brought the odd bouquet inside, she went to the bookcase in the parlor and pulled out Dover Publishing's tiny Kate Greenaway book: *The Language of Flowers*.

"Wild Licorice is the closest listing in here: 'I declare against you.' That's odd. Of all the anonymous bouquets, this is the first one that smacks of being sinister. Whoever is doing this must have been hard-pressed to find the herb, so he made a substitution, one I couldn't miss. That and I detest licorice." The strange bouquets started arriving the first time she had visited her folks, and came only when she was in Baysinger Cove.

"Who would know about this?" CJ took the book from her and thumbed through the sweet illustrations.

"Locally, Dotty Thystleberry would, but she's through harassing me now. There's always the Internet. I swear, if you can't find it online, you probably don't need to know it."

"That's a fact. The people who really hate you are behind bars and will be for a long time." CJ glanced at his watch. "We'd better head out now or we'll be late for church."

*****

After church, Maggie and CJ had a standing invitation for lunch with her mother and father at Eagles' Rest.

"There's a beef stew in the crock-pot, and it'll only take a few minutes to bake the biscuits," Larkin said, closing the oven door.

Sunday: a day of rest. Sitting still was anathema to her, yet she recognized that without such a day, she'd burn out fast. Siam purring around her ankles and Sheba's adorable soft brown eyes and wagging tail were welcome attentions today. Later, when she returned to the Cottage, Rusty and Tuffy would let her know she'd abandoned them and had been fraternizing with aliens.

After the lunch dishes were taken care of, they sat in the

Lake Room, watching the whitecaps frost the waves on Horseshoe Pond.

"Old Man Mountain is showing his age today," Larkin commented as she settled into her favorite chair. The deciduous trees that called the mountain "home" were shivering, bleak and bare, stripped of their autumnal glory.

"Those firs are huddled together as though they were holding a prayer meeting." Maggie claimed one of the big club chairs for herself.

"Waxing poetic, m'dear daughter?"

"Can't help it, daddy dear. The beauty of this place brings out the lyricist in me."

Rod smiled and looked very contented.

It was a cool day with meager bits of sunshine hovering behind heavy clouds. A haphazard mix of rain, snow, and fog were predicted for the next two days. The weather patterns had shifted, and the heavy snows and blizzards associated with New England winters were not expected now until late December. Much different weather than what she remembered from her schooldays—assuming her memory was not faulty. After all, that *was* a very long time ago.

"Wasn't that four-year-old girl the sweetest thing?" Larkin recalled the special music presentation before the Pastor gave his sermon. "Her little blue velvet dress really brought out the blue of her eyes."

"She hung onto her mother's skirt for dear life, but she wasn't shy about singing *Jesus Loves Me* all the way through. I loved her mother's flute accompaniment."

They talked about mundane matters while they drank cups of hot chocolate topped with marshmallow froth.

Maggie glanced out the big bay windows. A lacy flurry of delicate snowflakes fluttered down, acting much too lazy to become a blizzard, at least right this minute.

"We must plan our Thanksgiving celebration. It will be on us before we know it. First of all, we know who-all's coming for sure." Larkin set down her mug and put a legal pad on her lap. "We should decide who else we'd like to invite." She rummaged through the selection of pens and pencils that resided in a short cut-glass vase and selected a pen.

"This is my first holiday season in my home state with my own family. I wouldn't miss it for anything," Maggie got up and kissed her mother's soft cheek.

CJ cleared his throat, stood and walked over by the windows. "You know I usually spend the Thanksgiving weekend with my kids. This year, instead, I'll be here with y'all." He returned to the family circle. "Like Maggie said, I wouldn't miss it either."

"Oh, CJ, I do declare! That's so sweet." Larkin stood up and gave CJ a big hug. "Now, who else?" She settled back in her chair and retrieved her notepad.

Larkin was happy organizing a party of any kind. Though she and her sister had co-owned a very successful antique store in Georgia many years ago, Larkin could have chosen to be a professional party planner and been just as successful.

Rod said, "I saw Joshua and his wife at the Art Depot yesterday. Doing some early Christmas shopping, according to Damia. Should have but I didn't think to invite them."

"I'll do it, Rod. I need to talk to him anyway about the latest anonymous bouquet." Maggie described the licorice X and the dark red rose tied with a black ribbon, and its symbolism.

"An enigma, but still annoying," Larkin said, tapping her pen against her lower lip. "One of these days I hope your secret admirer reveals himself."

"I've got something to say to him," CJ said, his tone decisive and cold.

Maggie remembered that as a young man he was slow to anger, but capable of taking care of himself. "Don't think he's an 'admirer' as such, Larkin. In a way, I'd like to know, but I'm very uneasy about it."

Wanting to change the subject back to the more pleasant topic of holiday plans, Maggie asked, "What about your best friend Maisie and her husband?"

"Oh, that's a given. Remember Pastor Blessington's message this morning? He told us not to forget people who live alone, or small families in need of friendship and a helping hand."

"Quite true. Well, there's Dotty Thystleberry, and Harold at the bookstore," Maggie suggested. "What about Artesia Lovington?"

One day earlier in the month, while they were busy setting up the shop, Larkin had talked about the many crazy quilters in the area, especially Artesia Lovington. She was in her late seventies, sharp as the proverbial tack, and a dedicated crazy quilter. Her husband Rossiter had been an oil baron in Texas. When they retired here twenty years ago, they converted their summer home on Serenadelle Lake to a year-round domicile.

"Harold always comes. It's a standing invitation." Larkin

wrote their names down. "Artesia acts witchy sometimes, but she and Ross are alone. I'll call her. She is a sucker for a little bit of kindness. Their three children live out of state and pay absolutely no attention to their parents."

"They'll come around when the will is read, I'll bet," CJ said with a grin. "What about that sweet little apple-doll-faced woman, Sylvia L'Heure?"

"Sylvia has family in the area, so she spends her holidays with them."

"Our mayor is a widow now and has no children," Rod added. "And what about Pattysue and Kaleen?"

"We will ask. Since her husband's death, she's been spending holidays with her mom and dad. That's Henry and Audra Davidsby, you may remember, Maggie. Pattysue's cousin, Kevin Davidsby, owns the Sawmill Hill Cafe," Larkin said, her pen jiggling across the notepad.

Siam jumped in Larkin's lap and batted at the pen. "You little scamp! Shall I write your name down, too?"

"Mee-me-roo?"

"Yes, you too. I'll be sure to save some turkey just for you, little piggy." Larkin ruffled the cat's ears before he jumped down.

"I'm pretty sure she won't be going to the Morgans' house," Rod said.

Sheba, stretched out beside Rod's chair, snuffled and chased phantom rabbits in her sleep.

"Guaranteed fact," CJ agreed. "That's the last place Pattysue would spend the holiday."

"From what Pattysue told me some time ago, her folks never liked Bob Morgan. They only tolerated him at family gatherings for their daughter's sake." Maggie stretched every limb one at a time like a cat.

Siam hopped up on the arm of the chair and batted her hand, wanting to be petted. She pulled him down to her lap and complied.

"Our table service is for twenty-four; after that we would downscale to plastic, though I hate to do so for a holiday meal."

"Heaven knows we'll have enough food, no matter how many show up." Rod reached over and patted his wife's hand.

10

Monday, Monday

FOR ONCE, THE EARLY MORNING WEATHER FORECAST for snow showers was accurate. Sharp bits of icy sleet tap-danced at the window, softened by the kiss of tiny snow-flakes. The shop was closed on Sundays and Mondays, and opened at noon on Tuesdays. Mondays, Maggie planned to use as administration days: a dolled-up name for paperwork. So, she set about labeling file folders and the file drawers. Then she filed all of the invoices and catalogs that had arrived over the past month, which didn't take all that long to do.

She and the cats were snug and warm with the efficient geothermal unit purring along. The old oil-heat furnace had given up the ghost the very first week in November. Putting in the new system right away was the better plan. She was glad that the weather had cooperated for the digging to bury the water lines. And twice thankful that installing it had not interfered with their moving in and stocking the shop.

Ben Davenport's crew had built a new oversized two-car garage to replace the one that burned down in October. The big automatic overhead double door was being installed right now, so they would be done with this final last-minute project very soon. On the far left of the garage there was a standard-sized entry door. It provided access to the garage and cottage without having to open the big door. The garage was set back six feet from and eight feet away from the cottage. As soon as one entered the garage, to the left was a pass-through hallway to the kitchen, with doors at each end. Maggie used the wide passageway as a mudroom, where she kept her own winter boots and heavy coats. A small bureau corralled scarves, shawls, and gloves.

She picked up her checkbook and went downstairs with both cats trotting behind her. Hearing a tap on the mudroom door, she opened it to find Ben Davenport standing there.

"We're finally done, Maggie." Ben pulled off his gloves and reached inside his sheepskin-lined coat. "Here's the last statement of work on this job."

She wrote then handed him the check. "You've done a wonderful job with everything. If you ever need a reference, I'll be glad to write one for you."

"Thanks, Maggie. Ayuh, it's been a pleasure working for you. Never a dull moment around here." Ben's smile was reflected in his eyes.

"Hope your next job is more peaceful," she replied, matching his grin.

"It sure wasn't boring." Ben touched the bill of his trademark gimme cap and headed back out the door.

Three potted plants lived on the kitchen windowsill, gifts from green-thumbed Autumn. Well, they used to be *live* plants. Looking them over she was assaulted with the futility of the thing. She took the limp violet, the brown-leafed pothos, and the desiccated fern, pots and all, out to the garage and dumped them without fanfare into the trash. She had no talent for tending houseplants, no desire to play in the dirt, and didn't know why she kept trying. Lost cause. Brown thumb. Pesky weeds to some people were pretty wildflowers to her. A well-kept garden is a lovely thing—more pleasing if she didn't have to tend it. She loved the fir trees congregating all by themselves in the side yard. No fuss.

Autumn called, and they settled down for a nice chat. Maggie told her about the unceremonious funeral for the houseplants.

"Don't worry about it!" Autumn laughed. "Did you know Steve Longmaster died? You remember him. He was one of the Misfits."

"Like me." The Misfits were a small group of their classmates who were bookish, or quirky, like Steve, who was a whiz with numbers. "Where and when is the funeral?"

"It's Thursday at the funeral home in Aspen Grove. Maybe some other classmates will be there too. Want to go with us?"

"No, thanks, I'd better not. We never stayed in touch after graduation, so I don't really know Steve. Besides, I need to be at the shop."

Autumn understood and said how a funeral seemed to be a macabre place to reconnect with old classmates anyway. Then she changed the subject to talk about their upcoming trip to Florida.

"Chad and I will leave right after Christmas," she said, excitement coloring her words. "I hate the cold and snow."

"How long do you plan to stay?"

"At least until the end of March."

"Where? Have you found a place you like already?"

"I think so. Last spring, Chad and I flew down and looked at several cities. We like the Port Charlotte area. It is a nice little town, about halfway down on the Gulf Coast side. People are friendly since everyone is 'from away' down there."

Autumn went on to say that they would rent a place this time and look around for a mobile home park where they could buy. "Now that we are both retired, there's no reason to stay here."

"Never mind that I will miss you," Maggie scolded, yet she was glad for her old friends, that they could enjoy warmer climes instead of Maine's severe winter months.

"Oh! I have got to tell you a funny! I saw a road sign that actually said: 'When raining, turn on wipers and lights.' How stupid do they think Florida drivers are? Oh wait, don't answer that!"

They signed off. Still giggling, Maggie went online to check her e-mails. Sherrill, her friend in Oklahoma, sent an update on her new bead embroidery book: *Splendiferous Bead Motifs!* A preview copy was already on its way. On one of her frequent trips up to Stillwater for the Fifth Saturday play days, Maggie had seen the clever beaded examples that would be included in the book. She replied, offering congratulations and asking about wholesale terms.

Not wanting to miss anything, the cats followed her back upstairs to the bedroom. They watched every move as she unpacked several cartons of crazy quilt ephemera and organized the clear plastic boxes on the shelves in the small closet near her sewing area.

She came to two road-weary boxes. For whatever reason,

she'd schlepped them from house to house, without ever un-
packing them. Memorabilia. Memories better left buried in
their caskets of cardboard, dust, and duct tape. Her stomach
growled, reminding her it had been ignored since breakfast.
Once more, she dragged the boxes into the walk-in closet,
sliding them under the rod in the farthest back corner. Maybe
this would be the definitive move where she would open and
deal with whatever was stored inside. "*Mañana*. Not today."
Just call me Scarlett.

Her phone rang, and she ran to the bedroom to answer it.

"Hello, Maggie, me darlin'! And how's yourself this nasty mornin'?"

"Myself is fine, Maisie. What's up?"

"Old man weather may be changing his ways later, unless he changes his mind *again*. We are both busy women,
but would you join me now for a quick spot of tea? An hour
spent chatting with a friend over hot tea and warm crumpets
cannot go amiss."

11

Tea and Sympathy

THE O'REILLYS' WEE VICTORIAN COTTAGE was, truth be told, a large grand old Painted Lady. Her colors were muted, however: calm blue, gentle lavender, and soft green, with cream accents. Inside, the house was decorated in anything but the true Victorian style. It was light and airy with minimal distractions, things to trip over, or break. They sat in the living room on two very comfortable couches flanking the original ornate fireplace.

"What are crumpets?" Maggie asked as Maisie handed her a Dresden china plate with two crumpets and a fresh fruit medley on it. "I've never had one."

"They are akin to an English muffin, only softer," Maisie explained, handing her a jam pot.

Maggie slathered jam on each hot crumpet. "I thought these were a British staple, but you're Scottish." Spread with homemade strawberry jam, they smelled wonderful.

"We travelled the world, Maggie, me darlin', capturing the best delicacies from each country. We've very eclectic tastes."

"How do you make them?"

"Warm heavily-greased egg rings on the griddle. Then pour the batter into the rings. Release the rings a few minutes

57

later, flip the crumpets and in the blink of an eye, flip them onto your plate. Eat up, me darlin', before they get cold."

She took a bite, swallowed, and grinned. "I'm hooked!"

"Terrance will be pleased. He's the chief chef in our wee family, though I betake myself behind an apron now and again."

"Will he be joining us?"

"Not today. He's hung up his apron until dinnertime. For the between time he's holed up down in the cellar with some hush-hush project. He's no need to tell *me* to stay out of his workshop. I'd sprout fairy wings and fly before I'll ever take meself down those murderous stairs into that despicable dungeon." She shuddered then buttered another crumpet.

Maggie's shudder matched Maisie's. "Quite so. I detest cellars, too, all dank, dreary, and dismal with unmentionable critters in residence."

"Ah, 'tis not that bad, in truth. Terrance finished it off quite nicely for his den and workshop. It's those steep stairs I fear. Nasty!"

That subject out of the way, they changed conversational direction. They chatted about Maggie's first days in business during the dispatching of crumpets, fruit, and two cups of strong black tea.

"I love this room, Maisie. Did you do it?"

"Though I am an artist, me darlin', I cannot pull a room together to save my sainted mother's soul. Wayne's partner, Tony Leblanc, understood and helped me immensely. I wanted comfort and no fuss or frills."

"Oh, quite! There's more to life than housework." Maggie glanced around the room. "He did a good job."

"Any glimmer as to whodunit?" Maisie asked, wiping her mouth on a small tea napkin.

"Not a spark. Have you any ideas?" Maggie refilled her teacup and waved her hand to forestall another crumpet landing on her plate. "They are delicious, but I'm full."

"Nary a one. Tony's lifestyle may have bedeviled someone." Maisie shifted in her seat and looked into the middle distance. "Ah, it must have been at least three weeks ago. I was loading groceries in my car when I noticed Tony crossing toward the store. A big motorcycle with a scruffy old hell's angel astride it roared into the car park and made a straight run for Tony. Poor boy barely got out of the way in time. Nasty bruises from the fall, but he wasn't much hurt."

Other than the rider's general description, Maisie couldn't tell any more about the bike itself. "The bike was black and noisy. Machinery? Ha! I know when I turn a key the old beast starts. Beyond that I'm as lost as old Uncle Finnian MacDougal's fiddle—and that's a story for another day." Their talk turned to other things, and tea ended with the nickel tour of the house.

They were standing in Maisie's north-facing studio. Maggie looked around at several easels holding paintings in various stages of completion. "I am stumped as to what to give my folks for Christmas, Maisie. They have everything. Oh, I'll find something, maybe at the Art Depot."

"Aye, they may have everything. Now that you're here for keeps was the very best gift. Whatever you choose beyond that will bring them joy. Larkin adores chocolate, and Rod enjoys fine wine. Kasha makes the most delectable chocolates in this area."

"Speaking of wine and chocolate, Maisie, did you know Kasha is renting the empty half of her shop to a wine seller? 'The Vintner' will occupy the unused front room on the north side. They have replaced the front window with a door so people will have direct access from the street, or they can go from the wine room to the candy store by way of the interior door."

"Wonderful! The *Chronicle* no doubt will do a splash, so we'll take a peek then, shall we? We're a-comin' on Christmas, 'tis but a wee five weeks away."

"With your suggestion, I may be ready for it sooner than later. Since I'm here, please show me what you've been working on lately, then I won't bother you any longer."

"You be no bother, me darlin'. Come over here." Maisie stopped in front of an easel in the far corner of the well-lit studio and lifted the cloth. "I spied this beauty on Pemaquid Point in August."

Years of salt, sand, and wind had honed broken trees into artistic driftwood. Almost a perfect match, the two spires pointed skyward to the northwest like twin sentinels guarding the coast. A small brass plaque affixed to the driftwood frame gave the title: *Twin Sentinels*.

Maggie smiled. "Sold!"

12

Byways and Highways

MAGGIE STOOD IN FRONT OF THE OPEN PANTRY DOOR and sighed. Tea with Maisie had been a nice break, but her own cupboard, like old Mrs. Hubbard's, needed prompt attention. She loved to bake, and the smell of warm goodies was ambrosia. Not to mention needing groceries in general. "Tuna, pasta, granola, tomatoes, fruit ..." Two innocent furry faces looked up at her. "Nothing for it but a trip to the Mercantile," she told her feline audience. "Yes, I promise to get more kibble."

"Roo-roo!" Rusty said.

"Mee-rah!" Tuffy agreed.

The weather was leaning toward fog, but at least it was no longer sleeting. Maggie drove Camp Road north intending to catch the traffic light for a right turn at the busy intersection of Morrilton Road. About halfway there she spied a road off to the left with a signpost: Apple Spice Road.

Cute name. On a whim, she decided to take it. A few minutes later there was a sign indicating Appleton was seven miles ahead. That rang a bell. Her mother-in-law, Laura Irish Blue, had sent cards every Christmas, always with a post office box return address of Appleton.

Whoever plotted this road didn't have a passing acquaintance with the novel concept of a straight line. Granted, giant granite outcroppings, rolling rivers, and squiggly streams interrupt the best of highway plans. This wiggling byway gave a better understanding of "the path of least resistance."

Ghost trees rose up on each side of the road, mere shadows of what they were before winter's icy claws had stripped them of their dignity. Stately pines, firs, and cedars retained their verdant colors. Jolly red cardinals and bright blue jays flitted among the branches like animated Christmas ornaments.

Maggie crossed a short bridge over a sluggish stream. The skeleton trees were shrouded in veils of fog so thick she expected to be swallowed up if she got too close. Then with no warning she was enveloped in the clammy dampness. She dropped her speed down to a crawl until she crept out of the smothering fog bank.

Houses began to show up like abstract apostrophes between groups of trees. Though most of the houses looked forbidding and unwelcoming, she was glad to find herself in some semblance of civilization. She passed one cottage with that forlorn air of being abandoned. The only thing holding up the front porch was a whim and wishful thinking, and maybe not for long. The porch shuddered under the onslaught of a heavy wind gust. A long-forgotten plant pot went dancing a drunken tango down the broken stairs, spilling dust-dry dirt in its wake. *Nobody loves this house any longer. It's dying from a broken heart.*

The sun peeked out from behind a cloud. For a brief moment it glazed the needles of the pine tree and glistened off the broken windshield of a derelict car. A hawk swooped down, talons outstretched to snatch some unwary creature. He soared upward, successful in his quest, never once breaking his smooth gliding flight path.

Maggie came out of her abstraction and picked up her speed somewhat past turtle but not quite to rabbit. The road meandered through another copse of trees. Several crops of boulders, juvenile hills aspiring to be mountains when they grew up, caused the road to wiggle and veer northeastward. She hoped to connect with Morrilton Road soon or she'd have to turn around and backtrack.

Then she saw it. A small frame house was set quite close to the road. In the gravel driveway was a pristine 1967 green Dodge pickup with a metal-pipe push board in front of the grille. Parked beside the old truck was a motorcycle secured under a black canvas tarp.

For a moment her heart skipped a beat. She tightened her grip on the steering wheel as she slowed down. *Except for the push board, it was just like the truck Kiernan had. Oh, stop it! There's more than one truck like that in the world, silly!*

The dark, dusky pine trees are communal by nature. They plant themselves close together. When summer storms rage and winter winds blow, they huddle. The gentle spring breezes caress their boughs and they whisper love songs to one another. Today, they stood tall, silent, and unshakeable in their plot of *terra firma* located on the north side of the house.

The house was brown, tan, and dusty white. It looked like someone had gotten finger paints at the dime store and threw them on with a heavy hand. The front doorsteps resembled a dirty apron that was trying to disassociate itself from its owner, the porch.

An old man, bundled up in a dark blue pea coat and a pork-pie hat, sat in a rocker on the porch, smoking a pipe and watching Maggie's slow progress as she crept past. He raised his hand in the languid, one-size-fits-all, general Yankee greeting. She waved back and kept on going, increasing her speed to the posted limit.

Her cell chirped "Dixie." She pulled over to the roadside to take the call. "Hi, CJ, what's up?"

"Where are you?"

"Excellent question. Haven't the foggiest. Maybe you can help." Maggie told him the approximate location where she was, and the nonsensical reason why she'd taken the road less travelled. "Because it was there. Why else? But I came away without a map. Please tell me I can get back to town from here."

"Why didn't you use your GPS?"

"Um."

"Oh, never mind." He assured the technology-challenged Maggie that she could get there from here, and gave her explicit directions before signing off with a promise to catch up with her later and teach her, step by step, how to use the GPS. "It's not that difficult, *querida*."

If you say so. About a mile up the road she came to a T intersection and turned right, just like CJ had described. Sure enough, there was a sign for the Morrilton Road exit ten miles ahead.

She thought about her father-in-law, Emory Ira Blue. She

wasn't sure of his age. He might be close to saying *so long* to eighty, maybe even within hailing distance of ninety. When she talked to him on the phone, he always sounded strong. He did admit to a few minor health problems, which slowed him down. Losing Kiernan, his first-born, had been hard on him. Laura never quite got over it.

Now, caring for Kerrigan and his psychological problems was weighing heavy on the old man's heart. Emory had mentioned Kerrigan's massive head injury from a motorcycle accident three years ago. It seemed at times Kerrigan was two different persons, very mercurial.

Maggie promised herself to call Emory very soon. Perhaps he'd meet her at the Sawmill for breakfast one morning—without Kerry tagging along.

She'd met Kiernan's brother only once, and that was enough. Some people are born without some of their screws tightened down, or their moral wiring is scrambled. Kerry seemed to be the antithesis of Kiernan. Kerry had no conscience, no concept of right or wrong. Consequences did not faze him nor deter him from any goal he wanted. A very dangerous person is one who has no imagination to understand fear.

The sun casts its rays with benign impartiality on the poor and rich, the sane and insane, the just and unjust, as does the snow and rain. *Neither should I judge nor make comment, for truly, "There but for the grace of God," I could be.*

13

Soap Suds

THOUGH THE COTTAGE WOULD NOT OPEN until noon today, Tuesday, it had already proved to be a busy morning. "I'd like you to come every week to do all downstairs, Sammy. Every other week, please clean the upstairs, too." Maggie started to write a check for today's cleaning, but the house-keeper stopped her.

"I'll give you a bill at month end. Tuesday mornings are yours, then."

Samantha Sweeper was wife to Samuel, the chimney sweep. Sammy's cleaning company, Home-Swept, also did Eagles' Rest. Samantha was a no-nonsense gal with freckles and natural-curly red hair who tended to her business with little chatter, which Maggie appreciated, and said so.

Dottie Thystleberry tapped on the door just as Samantha went out.

"Come in, Dotty. What's in the bag?"

"Um, just some of my soaps." Her crooked smile was tentative and her pale blue eyes full of hope. "You said you wanted to try 'em."

"Yes, I did. Let's go in the kitchen. Want some tea?"

"How 'bout coffee?" Dotty slipped off her threadbare herringbone tweed winter coat and hung it on the back of the chair.

Maggie poured coffee into two stout ceramic mugs. Warm blueberry muffins with creamery butter also went over very well with Maggie's bashful guest.

Thanks to her father's and then her brother's old-fashioned notions of keeping womenfolk in the dark regarding finances, business, and the like, Dotty was not at all wise to the ways of the world. She was, however, a very talented grower of herbs, and gifted maker of natural soaps. There was precious little about herbs and natural oils that she didn't know.

Maggie's Cottage had once belonged to Dotty's family. Dotty had taken exception to Maggie's ownership of *her* home until Maggie's kindness had charmed the wizened old woman into acquiescence and friendship.

"Lavender, coconut, vanilla, roses. Oh, yummy stuff, Dotty. I'll take these four bars to start, please. Cash?"

"Please … and thank-ee."

Maggie gave her a twenty-dollar bill, and Dotty's eyes brightened. She dug in her pocket for change, and Maggie waved it aside. "My pleasure."

Dotty stuffed the money in her pocket and reached for another muffin. "You're a good cook."

"Thank you." She paused to take a sip of coffee. "My family is planning a big Thanksgiving celebration at Eagles' Rest. We'd be very pleased if you would join us."

Dotty looked up from buttering another muffin, her pale blue eyes wide with surprise. "You really mean it?"

"We really mean it. Please come."

"Thank-ee. I will." Her wrinkled face broke out in a

wreath of smiles. "Um, what's your favorite color?"

"Rainbow. Bright jewel tones and icy pastels like regal purple, cool blue, ruby red, rich black. Why?"

"Just wonderin'."

14

Bird Feathers

COOPER LARRADEAU AND PATTYSUE MORGAN came in and sat down at the kitchen table with their take-out lunches. Pattysue removed the deli sandwiches from the Stellar Bakery's paper bag. "The Crazy Club, oops, that's yours."

"Then this one's yours. What on earth is a Terrific Tuna Tizzy?" Coop asked.

"Tuna salad with a difference. Tuna, hard-boiled egg, celery, green onion, pimento, and sliced almonds, all mixed up with Miracle Whip. It's topped with barely melted Swiss and provolone cheeses."

"Sounds delicious," Maggie said.

Pattysue took a bite. "It is."

"I'll have to try that next time." Maggie put her own lunch dishes in the dishwasher.

"Thank you for helping me today. Coop."

"You don't need to thank me, Pattysue. You know I'll do anything for you," he said after swallowing a potato chip.

Yesterday, Pattysue's little yellow car that her late unlamented husband had called a "beached sunfish," floundered and went belly-up. She wanted to trade her husband's big black chrome-bedecked truck in for a vehicle more suitable for Maine's temperamental weather. This morning, her brother-in-law Cooper Larradeau had gone with her to a dealership in Augusta and helped her wade through the paperwork jungle.

"I got a year-old lease/purchase all-wheel-drive Subaru with low mileage. After the trade-in, there's not much owing on it, thankfully," Pattysue told Maggie.

"Congratulations. Sounds like you got a good deal."

"I did. And it's a pretty blue, too. My favorite color!"

Maggie went in the shop to straighten product that had migrated to other areas. She only heard bits and snatches of their conversation, which sounded like the continuation of an ongoing argument.

"You are beginning to sound just like Charlee," Pattysue argued, her voice rising in anger. "I like Harold, and I'm not going to quit on her say-so—or yours."

"I care about you. Kaleen is like my own daughter. I want her to have a father who'll love her and take care of her. I want to be her daddy."

"I know that, Cooper. But you'll always be Unk Coop to her ... you've been the big brother I never had—"

"I hear what you're not saying, Pattysue."

Maggie heard a chair scrape back and the trash hitting the large wastebasket in the corner.

"We're not through yet. I don't want you to regret this."

She scooted closer to the book display so it would not appear that she was eavesdropping. Not much chance of that, because Cooper never looked back as he stormed out the front door.

*****

"It's pretty quiet right now, Pattysue. I want to take some cookies to Harold. Do you mind watching the shop?"

"Nope. I'm good. I'll tag those new kits you made and restock the inventory."

"I have my phone if you need me."

The vintage sleigh bells jingled, announcing Maggie's entrance to The Happy Bookworm. "Hi howdy, friend!" She set a plate of cookies on Harold's desk.

"What's this?" Harold lifted the corner of the foil. "Smells delicious."

"Peanut butter cookies with chocolate chips."

"Oh, Maggie, my favorite. Thank you!"

The big brass cage that always sat on the corner of Harold's desk was empty. "Where's Chester?"

"He's flitting about in his playroom."

"Is he 'at home' today? I brought some nuts and fruit for him."

"Oh, he'll be so pleased. He's always up for visitors, especially bearing gifts. Come along then." Harold had found the very young bird after a big storm had battered the county several years ago. Because he had a fractured wing and could only flit short distances, Harold was given sanction to keep him. Being so very young, he learned to talk and showed more intelligence than one would expect from a crow.

The whole back porch was enclosed with combination windows making it an all-season room, except perhaps in the dead of winter. The floor tile was offset in a brickwork pattern. A wall of screening divided a third of the room, and a screen door gave access to Chester's playroom. Perches and pedestals of varying heights were scattered at random

71

throughout.

Together they went into Chester's playroom. Harold opened a small cupboard and removed two folding chairs. "Keeps them clean. Chester's not housebroken. The tile makes cleaning up a breeze." He opened the chairs and they sat down to watch Chester's antics.

Chester hopped from one perch to another before landing on the floor and walking over to Maggie. *"Hello, gorgeous!"*

"Hello, Chester. I'm Maggie."

He surveyed her with a beady eye. *"Magpie!"*

She laughed and repeated her name.

"Maggie! Maggie magpie!"

Harold shared Maggie's laughter. "It appears you have a new nickname."

"I hope not. Look, Chester, I brought you a treat."

"A treat! How sweet!"

"Would you like a walnut?" She held it out, balanced on the tips of her fingers. Chester cocked his glossy black head and came closer. He leaned in and took it from her with surprising gentleness.

He dropped the nut on the floor. Clutching it with his sharp talons and using his sturdy beak, he cracked it open with deft precision. After extracting the nutmeat, he flew up and landed in Maggie's lap. Surprised, she leaned back, hoping he wasn't eyeing her diamond stud earrings.

Chester dropped the nutmeat in her hand. *"Say I love you!"*

"I love you, too, Chester." With a light touch, she ran her hand down his sleek-feathered back.

"I love you!" He stretched up in the manner of a cat

arching its back when being petted. *"Maggie! Maggie magpie!"* He hopped down and ate the remaining nutmeat.

"I never realized how big crows actually were! For a second there, I thought he was going to feed it to me," Maggie said. "I'm very glad he didn't."

"He's never done that before. You've made a forever friend, Maggie."

"At this rate, my furred and feathered friends will outnumber my human ones!" She stood up, opened the bag and scattered the remaining nuts, seeds, and dried fruit in a tray resting on one of the short pedestals, tucking Chester's love offering in with them.

Harold put their chairs away, and they returned to the warmth of the bookstore. They settled in the reading nook with steaming cups of Earl Grey tea. "Have you been busy? Looks like you have, judging by the cars coming and going in your driveway."

"Quite busy. It surprised me, really. Without any history of course, I can't plot a trend line yet. How about you? You've been here quite a while."

"The week right before Thanksgiving, it's usually slow. Cookbooks are always popular this time of year, and holiday crafting books. Like you, I live above the shop so it's neither here nor there if I have customers or not. Don't misunderstand, of course I do want paying customers."

"Quite true. I'm pleased with my sales. Many were high-dollar purchases. Not too many of the penny-ante ones. Though it takes both to be successful. Old Ben Franklin said to 'Watch the pennies, and the dollars will take care of themselves.' It does all add up."

"That it does." He picked up a cookie, took a bite, and a look of pure bliss came over his face. "These are *so* good!"

"Thank you." Maggie smiled. "Marrying chocolate and peanut butter was serendipity squared."

"Speaking of adding up, I can't make any sense out of Tony's murder, much less *here* of all places." He finished his tea before reaching for another cookie.

"Convenience for the killer?"

"It certainly wasn't convenient for me." Harold shook cookie crumbs off his napkin into the wastebasket beside his chair. "It must have been premeditated if he came in here with a gun."

"The murderer was following Tony?" Maggie refreshed their teacups.

"Could be, or it's the universe's warped idea of malevolent serendipity. The person came in, saw a chance and took it, since Tony was killed over by the classic mystery bookcase. Outside would have made more sense. It would be highly preferable from my point of view," he sniffed. "Less chance of the killer being caught, too, I would imagine. Faster getaway."

"Murderers aren't as bright as they think they are."

"That goes without saying, Maggie. But why kill Tony Leblanc? What did he ever do to anyone, especially in this nice little town? Granted, I didn't care for the pass he and Wayne made at me. Even that's not a reason to murder him."

"Murder's not nice, period. One minute you're walking along, minding your own business. The next minute you're gone. No, murder is not nice." Maggie glanced out the window. Dusk was tiptoeing in, and she needed to get back to her own shop. The wind soughed through the pine trees and the venerable old Victorian home groaned, either from arthritis pains or she was talking to herself.

Harold rested his elbows on the arms of the wing chair and made a steeple with his fingers. "People need to make their peace with God *now*. Putting it off may be too late. Life can change in an instant. True, thankfully, no one knows when we are to die. Even with a fatal illness, there is some time to put one's affairs in order. Drop dead from a massive heart attack—no time. Murder—no time."

"I was saved in 1976, four years after I buried my husband. Before that, I had head knowledge of God's greatest gift. I searched the scriptures and gained heart knowledge. Two verses say it all, in my non-humble opinion: John 3:16, the gift of eternal life, and John 14:6, no equivocation."

"Well, Maggie dear, we certainly rode our theological hobbyhorses around the park this afternoon."

"That we did, my friend. I trust you are coming to Eagles' Rest for Thanksgiving as usual?" Maggie stood up and slipped on her coat.

"Wouldn't miss it. I'm making panettone this year."

"What's that when it's at home?"

"A better version of fruitcake. Don't wrinkle up your nose! It's really a sweet bread loaded with dried fruits, like apricots, raisins, pineapple, dates or cranberries, and walnuts or almonds. I vary the ingredients occasionally. It starts out as a yeast dough, not cake."

"Sounds yummy. I've never liked citron."

"Me, neither. Fortunately, Chester does. Oh, there's the bell. Maybe it's a real customer!"

15

Sweet, Sweet Talkin'

THE WEATHER HAD TURNED WARM for mid-November, in a relative sense. The sun was struggling to break through the benevolent clouds and show his full glory but couldn't quite pull it off.

Since Maggie had a space of free time before she opened the shop, she moved the birdseed container from the back porch and put it on one of the built-in shelves in the garage. It would be easier to fill the feeder here than being outside in the cold winter blasts that were coming just as sure as the sun would come up tomorrow. Whether Brother Sun would show his face today or sulk behind clouds was up for speculation. Earlier this morning she had opened the garage entry door to bring in fresh air.

She was opening a big bag of kitty kibble intending to also pour it in a lidded metal container when she heard the scritch-scratch of very small paws behind her. More than fresh air and daylight had taken advantage of the open door's invitation. Thinking it was a squirrel, she turned around, looked down, and stood stock-still.

The little creature's sleek black fur was interrupted by two long white racing stripes down its back. *Yikes!* The skunk cocked his head, and inquisitive eyes surveyed her. *At least he's facing me—now what?*

Pepé Le Pew's cousin was situated between Maggie and the back of the garage. Maggie was standing in its direct path to freedom. *Cat food? Would he eat cat food?* Her hand brushed her pocket, and she heard a faint jingle. Moving very slow in a non-threatening manner, she hoped, she reached in the pocket and brought out several bright shiny pennies. Somewhere she'd heard that skunks like bright things. *I hope. Or was that magpies? Too late to look it up now!*

With people, most always, if you don't look them in the eye when talking, they don't trust you. In the animal world, eye contact is a threat or a challenge.

Maggie sweetened her voice. "Good morning, Inky-Stinky-Pew. You have such a darling little face," she cooed. She dropped a penny and took a slow step back. "Oh, yes, you are a cute little thing." The skunk perked up and inched forward. "All bright-eyed and bushy-tailed this morning, aren't you?" Maggie now had her back to the open door. "Does your mama know where you are?"

Plink! Move one step back. "I thought y'all were night-owls, but you're an early bird, aren't you?"

Plink! Move one more step back. "How's the family?"

The skunk followed her out, step by plink-plink step. Still murmuring sweet nothings and having spent seven cents, Maggie was outside the door and moved away from the opening. The skunk looked up, blinked, saw freedom, and skittered off.

Maggie sighed, exhaling a long-held breath. Southern-belle sweet talk had once again saved the day.

16

Lively Lunching

AT NOON, CJ TOOK MAGGIE TO LUNCH at the Sawmill Hill Cafe. She had promised to bring sandwiches back for Rod and Larkin who were tending the Cottage while she was gone.

Maggie told CJ about her early morning adventure. "I never dreamed my Southern belle sweet talkin' act would ever be used to diffuse a close encounter with a skunk!"

CJ waggled his eyebrows. "I thought Southern sweet nothings was meant to encourage the male of the species, not discourage."

"It all depends on who, *what,* and when," Maggie said with a mock highbrow sniff.

CJ was still laughing when Shirley delivered their drinks.

"Larkin mentioned there's a mystery dinner theater at the community center the first Saturday in December. Do say that you'll go with me, please?"

"I don't really like *mystery* dinners," he said, deadpan.

It took a second for Maggie to catch the word play with the adjective. "It's not a *mysterious* dinner, silly. 'Did Stinky Don Varmint Bushwhack Sheriff Rick O'Shay?' is a dinner theater showcasing a hokey western mystery."

"Still—"

"The meal is western-themed. Barbecue, ranch beans, coleslaw, and corn bread. No road-kill."

"Well, maybe."

"If you're mumble-fussing about this, then why did you go with me to the one in Oklahoma City last spring?"

"To be with you, *querida*."

"So now that we're together most of the time, you don't want to go?" Maggie teased. "Come to dinner tonight. I'll make peach crumble for dessert."

"That's bribery."

"I know," she said. "Awful of me, isn't it? Dinner is at six-thirty. You will come, won't you?"

"I suppose so," CJ said, relenting with a grin. "Of course I will, *querida*. Even if you make tuna fish sandwiches."

Young Heather wore a happy smile as she delivered their lunches. "Look, Maggie!" She held out her left hand. A small diamond in a simple gold setting flashed out its hopeful promise.

"Who's the lucky guy?" CJ asked her.

"Jeremy White. His mom's the vet, Lisa Beecham-White. Her sister's the head librarian, Rebecca Blackpool. Old Hiram Beecham is their father and Jeremy's maternal grandfather."

Shades of the South: Who are your people? "Congratulations, Heather. I'm very pleased for you."

"Thank you." Heather refilled their drinks. She walked away, almost but not quite dancing, humming a popular love song.

Maggie ate a French fry, cooked extra crispy, just the way she liked them. "Fear not. It's a tangy chicken-broccoli casserole. If you don't like broccoli, I'll use asparagus."

CJ poured a puddle of ketchup on his plate. "I like broccoli if it's disguised."

Two people, whom Maggie didn't know, were sitting in the booth across from theirs, and almost finished with their meals.

"What on earth are we going to do about Kaleen, Audra?"

"What do you mean, Henry?"

Ah, Pattysue's parents, Henry and Audra Davidsby. I'd best keep my ears open.

"Charlotte wants custody."

"It'll be a cold day before that happens." Audra finished her soft drink.

"So, what can we do? Abscond with her?"

"Don't be silly, Henry."

"It's not that silly. Kaleen is five going on nine. Incredibly smart—must take after me."

"Of course, dear. But she's still a baby to me."

"Smart little britches, she'll be a handful. Remember our girls at that age? Especially Pattysue. You want to raise another one?" he reached across the table and held her hand.

"I'd love the chance, you know that." Her tone was wistful.

"Okay, Audra, here's what we'll do …"

The flurry of a young family of three, coming to sit down in the booth behind CJ, drowned out the rest of Henry's plan. *Razzlefratz!* Maggie returned her attention to her meal.

"Do you think Linda and Ron will marry each other *again*?" the man asked his wife.

"They're too old," the young boy said from his unique perspective. He looked and sounded like a seven-year-old.

His mother laughed. "You're never too old to get married."

CJ cocked his eyebrow at Maggie and grinned, the ends of his mustache pointing to the dimple that always set her heart a-flutter.

"I don't like girls now," the youngster stated with all the conviction of his tender years. "Can I wait to get married in heaven?"

Maggie and CJ were at the bakery counter picking up their take-out orders when the young family came up to the register behind them.

The well-mannered but loquacious little boy was still asking questions. "Did you have M&Ms when you were young, Dad?"

Once assured that those candies were around, even *way back then*, the boy posed a deeper question. "Who was Jesus's grandfather?"

"God is Jesus's father. There's no one else except God," his mother explained, her face perplexed as if wondering from whence this inquisitive child had come.

"No. I mean Joseph's father."

17

The Joys of Retail

WHEN THEY RETURNED TO THE COTTAGE, Maggie said she'd take care of the shop while Rod and Larkin ate their lunches in the kitchen. She left them still talking about the scarcity of clues as to who murdered Tony Leblanc when the door chime rang and several women came in together. She shut the Dutch door and followed them into the shop.

One woman asked if there was a kit for making a crazy quilt. She was thin, dark-haired and talked nineteen to the dozen. She went from one section to another, enthusing about the wide range of selection the shop offered. Her companion was quieter and busied herself looking over the ribbons and trims displayed in the old armoire.

Maggie caught up with her at the book display wall. "The quilt is hanging in the classroom if you want to see it. I designed it especially for folks transitioning from the world of sane quilting into the arena of crazy quilting where rules do not apply. It's called 'Simply Crazy' and can be paper-pieced or stitched to a muslin foundation."

"What's in the kit?"

"Complete instructions, the block schematics, the fabrics, all of the trims and beads, perle cotton, silk ribbon, needles and thread. Everything's included but the sashing and border fabrics because not everyone likes the blue I used."

"Where's the kit and how much?"

"Right here." She pulled a kit from the stack on a shelf. "It's two hundred and fifty dollars. My design, limited edition of ten kits."

"It's very pretty. How many have you got?"

"Only six."

"Five. I want one."

"Four. I want one, too!" her friend piped up. "What else can we get in trouble with here, Donna?"

"You've got to see the lace appliqués, Diana! Oh, look at these lovebirds framed in a heart—they're darling. And the puppy! It's adorable!"

Rod came in and stepped behind the cash desk. "Larkin is cleaning up the kitchen," he informed Maggie. "She'll be in shortly."

Three more customers came in together, each carrying a tote bag already somewhat stuffed. They browsed around, chattering back and forth. Maggie noticed that more and more people were carrying cloth shopping tote bags.

"If it helps to conserve our resources, it's a great concept. If it aids shoplifting, it's not great from the retailer's standpoint," she murmured to her father.

Maggie got buttonholed with a question about the washfastness of certain trims.

"When in doubt, test a small bit first. Wet a paper towel then lay the trim down. If color shows up, there's your answer: not a good idea to wash it."

"Makes sense. Thanks. I'm gonna look around some more." She shrugged her large heavy-looking tote bag up onto her shoulder then wandered off to join her friends over by the kits. They conferred for several minutes, keeping their voices very low.

Rod was in his element, chatting up the ladies as they paid for the crazy quilt kits and a stack of additional pretties. His left arm, broken in a non-accidental fall down the metal stairs at Eagles' Rest a few weeks ago, was still in a cast. He couldn't do much to help in the shop itself, but he was a wizard with technological gadgets. Maggie, though conversant with the mechanics of running the cash register, was more than happy to delegate that job to him.

Diane asked a complicated question about paper-piecing the blocks for the kit she had just purchased. While Maggie was explaining, she noticed the other three women leaving without buying anything.

"If you get stuck, call. I'll set aside a special time to walk you through it," Maggie offered, thinking she might schedule a complimentary class for all the people who had bought this kit.

"Oh, that's awfully nice of you," Diane said.

Diane and Donna left together, chattering about the fun they were going to have working on the crazy quilts. Maggie heard Donna say as they walked to the hall, "Why don't you come to my house Saturday ..."

For the moment, the shop was quiet. Maggie straightened up the remaining crazy quilt kits, but something didn't look right. The kits were packed in clear expandable twelve-inch square envelopes, and were about three inches thick. Sure enough, instead of four, only three kits remained on the shelf.

"Razzlefratz!" she mumbled as she went to join her father who was replenishing the big shopping bags.

"What's the matter?"

"Some benighted *person* stole one of the crazy quilt kits. I'll bet it was that last group of women who didn't buy anything. One of them distracted me and you were busy at the checkout."

Rod's jade green eyes darkened to malachite. "Classic theft maneuver."

"It was bound to happen sooner or later. I'll call Kenny Watts. I hate to do it. I'd like to trust my customers, but that's not possible in this day and age."

"That's a sad epitaph."

"It is that. I need a security monitor or something in here."

"Technology has improved tremendously. I'm not sure, but you may be able to access the cameras from your cell phone," techno-savvy Rod said with a happy grin. "I'll call him, if you'd like."

Seeing the gleam in his eye, Maggie agreed that he'd be the better one to make that particular call.

Pattysue came in, unzipping her parka. "I know I'm not scheduled to work today. There's nothing to do at the bookstore. Is it okay for me to hang out here until Kaleen gets off the bus?"

"Of course. And you know that any hours you work here, you'll be paid, scheduled or not."

"Thanks, Maggie. I sure can use the money. Kaleen's growing so fast I can barely keep clothes on her these days." She hung her parka in the hall closet and came back in the shop.

"My parents, Coop, and Charlee all seem to want to take over. So far, I'm doing okay all by myself."

18

More Joy

THERE WAS A LULL BETWEEN CUSTOMERS, so Pattysue and Maggie went to the kitchen for a tea break. They left the top half of the Dutch door open.

"I honestly don't know what to do," Pattysue moaned as she picked up a rich dark chocolate brownie. "Charlee threatened to sue for custody of Kaleen if I don't do what she wants. In one breath she tells me to quit the bookstore. Don't get married, especially to Coop, but it's okay to date Doc Grayson with marriage in mind. Then in the very next breath, she says how much she would have to sacrifice if she did take on the raising of my daughter. She's such a martyr. She's making me nuts! I hate to listen to such negativity. Some days it's harder to ignore her than others."

"You're doing fine. Don't let her pessimistic comments shipwreck your day and drown your dreams. You work two jobs, and I cannot see that Kaleen is neglected in any sense of the word. I can vouch for that."

"I know that, Maggie, but Charlee never has liked me. She called me a schemer and accused *me* of leading Bob down the path to his destruction. According to her, her baby boy would never have been a drunk, a liar, and a batterer, if I hadn't driven him to it. He was a drunk before I married him.

I found out about his lies later. Now she's on the warpath, complaining about my friendship with Coop, the husband of a murderer—my sister's ex-husband. It's not like murder is a contagious disease."

"And what does Coop think about all this?"

"He claims he's not homophobic, but he really doesn't like my working at the bookstore either, even though I've told him Harold is straight. He really wants me to be a stay-at-home mom. I'm not sure what he means. His mistress? I don't think so!"

"Tell me this isn't straight out of a bodice-ripper dime-store novel, is it?" Maggie asked, grinning. Neither she nor her young friend favored the so-called women's fiction or romance novels for a cozy read.

"My little house is paid for, thanks to that life insurance policy Bob had. That's fine, except there's oil and utilities to pay, not to mention food and clothing. Even if I planted a quarter in rich soil, it wouldn't give me a money tree."

The shop phone rang and Pattysue went to answer it. A scant minute later she said, "Oh, I am so glad you called! Great timing! ... Yes! You have won a seventy-five-inch state-of-the-art home entertainment center! ... Absolutely free! I need your credit card information for the shipping costs ..." Pattysue hung up. "Well! That was rude. He hung up on me."

"That was hilarious, Pattysue. I never thought about turning the tables on a sales shark. Who was that, anyway?"

"Selling something, I'm not sure what. He didn't speak the same English I speak."

"The other day I had an email order for a book to be sent

to England. When I called the lady, it was at least twenty minutes before I could get her credit card number straight. Bless her, she was probably just as frazzled as I was, but we managed. Two English-speaking countries separated only by a common language and an ocean! Dialects, accents, regional slang, and idioms are the epitome of frustration—theirs too, probably, wading through *our* idiosyncratic language. Give me e-mail, the printed word, or dare I suggest a *written* letter—such a novel idea! Some days I really hate talking on the phone."

"It can be a challenge." Pattysue glanced at her watch. "Oh, I've got to go. Are you sure you don't mind watching Kaleen until I get back from the dentist?"

"Not to worry. She's a good girl and we'll stay busy. I'll make my favorite 'Not Your Mama's Mac and Cheese' for dinner tonight. You *will* eat with us—and don't argue. You surely won't want to cook when you get home."

"A grown-up version? Sounds yummy."

"Yes, with eight different cheeses, and penne pasta."

"Sounds good to me, too. Am I invited?" CJ asked as he hung his coat in the hall closet.

"Madame" entered and followed him into the shop. She was the current president of the Quilt Society. Harriet Bellingrath was a quilter as well as a beaded-jewelry maker. She looked around before she said, "I have no desire whatsoever to embellish quilts with beads. *Tedious*. I *only* use the best hot-fix crystals on my *prize-winning* art quilt wall hangings."

Tedious only if you don't like doing it. Labor-intensive? Yes. A little bit of Madame went a long way. "We have all of the Swarovski colors in three sizes."

After the last Quilt Society meeting, Larkin had told Maggie about Harriet. Imperious and autocratic were the more polite personal adjectives applied by most people she met, hence the nickname. When Harriet first heard it, as Birdie's news-vine story went, instead of being put out, she felt it was a compliment and adopted it as her moniker.

Though Harriet was of average height, she held herself rigid as if she were still balancing a book on her head to maintain correct posture. This gave her the appearance of being taller.

She stood in front of the rack of beads while Maggie was behind the cash desk adding paper to the printer tray.

"My brother-in-law, Alex, is married to your cousin Susie."

"Really? Small world. Can I help you find something specific, Madame?"

"Oh, don't 'Madame' me. Today, I'm just one of the girls, out shopping for beads." The la-di-dah in her voice almost put Maggie into a giggle fit.

Madame hadn't been a "girl" for a half-century or more. Maggie smiled and bit her lip trying hard to contain the giggle.

CJ looked heavenward and cleared his throat, covering his mouth to hide a laugh as he sat down in one of the visitor chairs.

Harriet pulled a popular beading magazine out of her capacious purse. Multi-colored slim sticky notes bristled above the glossy pages like a Technicolor porcupine. She found what she was looking for and folded the magazine open and back on itself. "I want to make this amulet pouch."

"Do you want Czech seed beads or Delicas?" Maggie asked. She came around the cutting table and walked over to the bead wall with Harriet.

"What's the difference?"

Maggie showed Harriet two necklaces, both created from the same pattern. "This was made on a loom with the precise Japanese cylinder beads called Delicas. It has a tighter weave, giving the 'fabric' a supple grace. This one is peyote stitch and is made from seed beads. It's larger overall and has the traditional bumpy texture of Native American bead-work."

"You of all people should know 'peyote stitch' isn't PC. It's a 'gourd' stitch. And shouldn't you say: 'First Americans'? We must be PC these days," Harriet sneered in her autocratic voice.

Certain things didn't take much to set Maggie's quicksilver temper flaring. "Many different names have been used to refer to the indigenous peoples of the Americas, of which *I* am one. 'Native American' is accepted by the US government." Quarter Cherokee herself, Maggie was non-politically correct down to her core, but even she liked the government's term better than the generic "Indian."

Madame looked like she was about to say something else rude, but seemed to think better of it when she looked at Maggie. She tossed her red knitted scarf back over her shoulder in an imperious manner.

What is it with red fuzzy accessories all of a sudden? Did I miss something? Probably. She cared not for fashion as such, only if it looked good on her and she liked it.

91

"Whose design is this?"

"Mine. All of the patterns and kits in the shop are my own design."

"Well, aren't *you* the clever one?" Her tone suggested the compliment was forced. "Of course I want only the *best*. My time is precious and I demand perfection." Her nose was so high in the air she wouldn't see a nasty before she stepped in it. Madame may have dropped the moniker today but not the attendant attitude.

"Quite." Maggie led Madame over to the Delica beads. "They are displayed in the colors' numerical order. Most patterns list the color number along with the name. Numerically it's easy to find what you want."

Madame must have taken a bath in the bordello-like perfume she wore. The scent combined with the woman's personal chemistry created a particular odoriferous equation. By now it had arrived to the point of setting Maggie's olfactory senses off. She sneezed five times in rapid succession then trotted over to the cash desk for several tissues to stop the immediate fall-out.

Madame set her tray, close to overflowing with beads, on the counter. "Allergies? They have drugs for that, you know."

19

Odds Are

DINNER WAS EXCELLENT, both the food and the company. Using a sliced loaf of French bread, CJ made Parmesan cheese and garlic toast. Larkin created a mandarin orange salad tossed with slivered almonds on a bed of baby spinach leaves and drizzled it with raspberry vinaigrette. Both were perfect accompaniments for the gourmet mac-and-cheese casserole. Kaleen, with Maggie's help, contributed cupcakes. Kaleen had announced with pride that she frosted them, which, of course, enhanced the cupcakes' reception.

Later that evening, she and CJ sat in the parlor reading in companionable silence. He was halfway through a Dean Koontz thriller. In the background, Jim Galway's soulful clarinet was a gentle counterpoint. By tacit agreement they shelved the current mayhem and murder in exchange for the fictional versions.

Maggie, snuggled up with an Anne Perry mystery, was engrossed in the middle of a cliffhanger chapter when, out of the corner of her eye, she caught sight of a critter skedaddling as fast as eight legs could carry it. In one fluid motion, she flew off the couch, grabbed a flyswatter from under the coffee table, and gave the repulsive intruder a hearty swat. Next thing she knew, she was topsy-turvy, wedged between the loveseat and the coffee table. "Owww, ouch!"

Both cats took off, running for higher ground, thundering up the stairs, fussing all the way.

"Are you okay? Just what *are* you doing?" CJ stood over her and extended his hand to help her up.

"Spider warfare." She looked at the corpse clinging to the flyswatter and shuddered. "Maggie, one. Spider, zero."

"Better odds than the sheriff is having with finding Tony's killer. He hasn't unmasked your Lone Ranger yet, either. He and Abigail went to the Masquerade Ball last Friday. There were several masked men there, but none matched your description and none of them limped."

"A limp can be faked, of course. Why he targeted me and my customers with his terrible theatrics is beyond me."

20

Sweet Nothin's

MAGGIE CUDDLED UP TO CJ on the loveseat with her head on his shoulder. *Where it fits quite nicely, thank you.*

Rusty stretched out on the arm of the couch next to CJ, while Tuffy was snoozing beside Maggie.

"Here we are, one happy family." Maggie stifled a yawn. "Can't beat that with a stick, as Grandfather often said."

"No, we can't." CJ leaned down and kissed her head. She moved so their lips met for a long, lingering, languorous kiss.

A few minutes later, his voice husky, CJ asked, "Where will we put everything? My cottage isn't all that big."

Maggie disentangled herself from his embrace. "It's plenty big enough ... wait a minute! What are you planning that I don't know about yet?"

"Marriage."

"You haven't formally asked me yet."

"I have." He pulled her back down beside him.

"When?"

"Let's see. Last year. Your silver pen was the key that opened the door to finding my long-lost high school sweetheart. And at Christmas when I caught you under the mistletoe at Eagles' Rest. Now."

"Now, what?"

"Now, we're discussing marriage, *querida*."

"I love you more than life itself, CJ. I'll never marry anyone but you, when I do marry."

"You don't know how much I care for you, *mi corazón*, in case you hadn't noticed."

"Oh, I *have* noticed." She snuggled into his neck, smelling the herbal soap and Stetson aftershave he favored. "We're both hat over boot heels in love with each other."

"Should we buy a bigger place? I can add on to my cottage. I've got acreage enough." CJ shifted position, and Rusty took off.

"Can we wait until after the holidays?"

"Sure. Sunday, January second."

"Sunday?"

"After church. Invite the whole congregation, if you want to."

"Sunday, January second?"

"Quit talkin' and kiss me."

21

The Plot Thickens

MAGGIE WAS BUSY WITH THE LAST SALE of the day so Pattysue answered the shop's phone. "What? Mrs. Sanger, calm down! What are you saying? … What happened?"

Maggie escorted her customer out, turned off the "Open" sign, locked the front door then hurried back. One look at Pattysue's stricken face and Maggie knew there was trouble ahead. "What's wrong?"

Pattysue dropped the phone back in the cradle, her face as white as the snow drifting down outside the shop's front window. "K-Kaleen's gone!"

"Gone?" Maggie echoed.

"Missing!" Pattysue wailed.

"Lord-a-mercy," Larkin said, reverting to her Southern roots. She steered Pattysue to the kitchen. In short order, the distraught young mother was sipping a cup of hot sweet tea.

Between sobbing hiccoughs, she related the upsetting news. "Because of Scotty, Kaleen wanted to stay with Mrs. Sanger after school today. They were outside playing with him …" She trailed off and stopped to blow her nose.

"Who's Scotty?" Maggie asked.

"Mrs. Sanger's new little black Scottish terrier. He saw a chipmunk and took off behind the house after it. She went after the puppy, thinking that Kaleen was right behind her. She said it took her less than five minutes to catch him. When she went around front, Kaleen wasn't outside, or inside. She wasn't anywhere! Oh my God! Where's my little girl?"

In between the sobs, Maggie convinced the worried mother they'd best call the sheriff. "I'll do it, Pattysue." She pulled her cell phone out of her pocket and hit the speed-dial number for the sheriff's phone. Afterward, she drove Pattysue's car, taking the panic-stricken woman home where the sheriff had said he would meet them.

*****

"No ransom note or phone call?" Sheriff Walker Bainbridge asked Pattysue, his voice gentle but firm. They were gathered in Kaleen's little bedroom. The wallpaper was a plethora of pink roses and trailing vines. White-painted furniture and ruffled pink gingham curtains at the lone window completed the very sweet girlie room. On the bed, two dolls were napping on Kaleen's pillow. A small doll quilt was tucked around them.

"Not yet … " Pattysue gulped down a sob. "No message on the answering machine, either."

"Anything missing? Clothing, toys?"

Pattysue rummaged through the bureau then ransacked the closet. "Her pink suitcase is gone. A few clothes, but that's all. Her dolls are right where she put them this morning." She backed up to the canopied twin bed and almost tripped. Teddy was under her foot, Kaleen's beloved care-worn bear. With trembling hands she picked it up and smoothed out the red satin ribbon around his neck. She sat down on the bed, rocking back and forth, clutching the bear to her chest. "S-she wouldn't have gone anywhere without T-Teddy." Tears ran down her cheeks like raindrops rushing to meet the sea.

Maggie sat down on the bed and hugged Pattysue. Words were superfluous now. She brought to mind a Native American saying from the Minquass Tribe, that the soul would have no rainbow if the eyes had no tears.

A few minutes later, Maggie made coffee and they sat around the scarred white enamel table.

Pattysue was calmer, in between heavy sighs. "Our Young Adult Ministry lesson last Sunday was about praying like everything depends on it. Then to take action like it depends on us to get going and follow through." She sipped coffee before continuing. "God will keep me strong through this. So, sitting around moping won't do any good. Not for her or me. Must tell my parents. I'd better call Charlotte first to see what she has to say, too. She needs to know, I guess."

She put the bear in the empty chair beside hers then picked up the kitchen phone and dialed. "There's no answer at home. I'll try her cell," she said, dialing again. "Oh, hello, Charlee ..."

Fifteen minutes later, Pattysue related the gist of the phone call. "She sounded concerned about her 'baby' but she seemed awfully distracted. She told me everything's okay ... I think that's what she said. There was so much static on the line, I couldn't hear her very well. She said there was a storm coming in, causing the bad reception." She glanced out the window and frowned. "That doesn't make sense. All of Baywater County is supposed to have nothing but flurries today. Not enough to matter." She sighed. "Oh, I'd better call my parents."

"Today's phones aren't usually subject to the vagaries of storms, unless the power lines go down," Maggie said to Walker while Pattysue was phoning her folks.

"Unless there's stuff going on in the background, like a motor running, a power saw, or something just as noisy where you can't hear yourself think, maybe," the sheriff replied.

"Are you all right here by yourself?" Maggie asked when Pattysue sat back down at the table.

Pattysue picked up the bear and hugged it tight. "Yes. Kaleen would call me here first. She hasn't learned my new cell number yet. You heard me tell my parents not to come, as much as they insisted. Roy is on duty at the Clinic tonight. I'll call Cooper, he needs to know, too."

"He's still living in Willow Grove, isn't he? That's not far from here," the sheriff said.

Pattysue nodded, dialed, and left a message. "That's strange. He didn't say he was going out of town."

"What do you mean?" the sheriff asked.

"Last time we talked he sounded like he was going to be home. He wanted to get caught up on some paperwork before Thanksgiving. The message on his machine says he'll be out of the office for a week, beginning today." She paused then elaborated. "After he divorced Carrie, he closed his accounting business in town. He has an office at home now."

"Cooper's really fond of Kaleen, isn't he?" Maggie

100

asked.

"He always has been. Carrie never wanted kids of her own."

The sheriff stood up, stretched, walked to the sink and looked out the window. "Who has keys to your house?"

"Keys?" She looked as if she were remembering the other time keys were the pivotal clue to solving a mystery—the one that put her sister in jail for double murder. "Um, Dad has one. Mrs. Sanger, in case Kaleen needed something before I got home from work, or I locked myself out." Her rueful grin suggested she had done just that a time or two. "If Cooper has Carrie's keys, then he's got one now. Charlee? I suspect Robert may have given her a set but I sure didn't, and wouldn't."

"Pattysue, would Cooper Larradeau take Kaleen?" the sheriff asked, turning around to face her.

"She'd go willingly with him. Kidnapping her would end any chance I'd ever marry him. Doesn't make sense. Married to me or not, he can still see her whenever he wants to." She petted the care-worn teddy bear. "He gave this to Kaleen for her third birthday."

"Would he do it to scare you?" Maggie asked.

"Why would he?" Pattysue thought for a long moment.

"He could argue that Kaleen's not safe unless he's around," Maggie said.

"But if he's got her," Pattysue replied, "she's old enough to tell the truth, no matter who took her."

"It's kidnapping. Period," the sheriff said, standing up. "Someone she knows, if her suitcase is gone, too."

Maggie joined him at the door.

Pattysue said in a small voice, "I don't know if Cooper would or not." She put a hand over her face, letting the tears drip across her fingers. "I'll be okay alone. I'll call if I hear … if I need … anything."

22

Slip-Slidin'

BACKLIT BY THE STREET LIGHT, the oak tree in the front yard, clenched in winter's icy grip without one leaf to bless itself with, bowed under the blanket of white crystals doing acrobatics on their way down. The snow wasn't supposed to accumulate, but it was doing a good imitation of a blizzard in the making. In Maggie's non-humble opinion the weather people ought to look out the window every so often, like she was doing now. The forecasts might be a tad more accurate.

CJ's pale blue SUV, which he drove in inclement weather rather than his big truck, "Miss Dixie," swerved into the driveway. She heard the garage door rising then descending a few moments later. Both cats barreled downstairs.

CJ came in through the passageway into the kitchen carrying a brown paper shopping bag. The cats were running the gauntlet between his legs. "Hey guys, let me at least get in, will you?" He set the bag on the counter then enveloped Maggie in a bear hug and gave her a heart-warming kiss. It was a bit tricky with two cats pawing at their knees.

"It's getting as slippery as a snake on skates out there." CJ chafed his hands together to get them warm before taking his coat to the hall closet.

"You can stay here if the roads are bad." The loveseat in

her sitting room folded out into a very comfortable twin bed. She had slept on it one night, expecting the delivery of her mattress and bedframe first thing the next morning.

"I know that, *querida*. We'll check the weather later."

CJ kept a change of clothes here, as did Maggie at CJ's home. Winter weather can interrupt and rearrange the best-laid plans. Some time ago they had also exchanged keys, for safety and convenience. That was a leap of faith for Maggie, but she trusted CJ.

The basics of the person you truly are, never change. Adopted behaviors and learned attitudes, join with life's vicissitudes, which add an unknown factor in the equation. The intervening years between childhood and now were but intermittent pauses in life's movie, with many scenes long forgotten.

Would she have stayed married to Kiernan if he'd returned alive after his last tour in Viet Nam? He was talented, often impatient, sometimes claiming an artist's temperament for his mood swings or when he had the adult version of a tantrum. Maggie had interpreted it as being the spoiled brat syndrome. Would they have weathered the distance of years, becoming reacquainted and made stronger in spite of the radical changes wrought by war's storm?

So, what brought on this wee bit of introspection? A premonition? Kiernan's dead. CJ is the man in my life right now, and I like it just like that.

"I didn't think you'd want to cook or go out tonight, so I brought dinner. Fish and chips, still hot from the Sawmill Hill Cafe's kitchen," her true love said.

"You must be a mind-reader. Thank you, dear heart. I

suspected it was fish by the way these two beggars are dancing."

"I know better, so I brought extra."

"Good thing. You are now their new best friend!"

CJ once again enveloped Maggie in a big hug, and they shared a sweet kiss.

After that brief interlude, CJ broke a piece of fish in half, divested it of its breading then divided the portion onto two paper plates. Almost before he could set them on the floor, two furry noses with whiskers a-twitching were buried in the plates.

"Does Walker have any leads on Tony's murder?" Maggie asked. "I haven't seen him for a while. I've been incredibly busy. Way too busy to do much asking around."

"Did you know he traced the gun? It's registered to Robert Morgan."

"But he's dead!" Maggie stated the obvious. "So what happened to his effects? Pattysue inherited, of course. I would have thought she'd cleaned his things out long before now."

"With an inquisitive young child in the house, I'd hope the gun was well secured," CJ replied.

Maggie set two plates and tableware on the table. "If Pattysue had found it, she certainly wouldn't have shot anyone, especially Tony Leblanc. Maybe she would have shot her abusive husband, except her sister got there first. I wonder where all his stuff went? Could be Charlotte took it all. She might have taken his gun home with her, citing the child's safety. It would be just like her."

"I saw the sheriff for a few minutes at the Sawmill." CJ

portioned out the fish, the flash-fried potato chips, and tartar sauce. "Yesterday he pulled Wayne Hardy in again for questioning. Wayne grew up in the really bad part of Chicago. There were so many gangs, some with such deadly vendettas against gays that he barely survived, and almost didn't. One night, a bunch of thugs beat him up and left him for dead. After a long recovery, he moved here hoping Baysinger Cove would be more tolerant. Wayne abhors violence. As Walker said before, Wayne's prints aren't on the trigger. There are no other prints on the gun so the shooter wore gloves."

"Would Wayne have taken Kaleen?" Maggie asked after swallowing a forkful of flaky cod.

"I hardly think so." CJ paused to eat a still-warm potato chip. "By his own admission, children are not his favorite people. They are too perceptive, I reckon."

"Then who took her? What does Tony's murder have to do with the kidnapping?"

"That, my Maggie, is the crux of the matter."

23

Retrospection

STACCATO BURSTS OF HAIL TATTOOED the sitting room window like shotgun pellets, ripping the fragile fabric of memory. Maggie hated hail; more so the image attached to it.

*****

In April 1972, a hailstorm pelted the tent that had been erected over the rectangular hole in the ground. Relentless bits of icy sleet mixed with dime-sized hailstones slipped through and peppered the bearers waiting to lower Kiernan Irish Blue's coffin.

She was numb with cold, and tears froze on her cheeks as she stood shivering between Rod and Larkin. Colonel Rod Richardson was dressed in his Air Force uniform. Larkin wore a heavy black winter coat over her dark blue dress suit.

Maggie looked up. On the other side of the grave, Emory and Laura Blue stood, huddled together against the cold, clinging to one another in sorrow, as they watched their son be buried. Beside them and a little ways apart, a Marine stood at attention and snapped a salute as the coffin was lowered into the gaping maw that would swallow it whole. Dust to ashes. Ashes to dust.

Staring at the lone Marine, her heart was in her throat. *Kiernan? No!*

Rod caught her arm as she started to sway. "I'm ... okay," she whispered.

A Marine in dress blues wearing the insignia of a Major approached carrying the tri-folded flag. Facing the giant Marine standing in front of her, she received the flag and clutched it to her chest. The Major stepped back and saluted.

The lone soldier was no longer there on the other side of the grave. The incident spooked her, and she never forgot the brief glimpse of a man who could have been her dead husband's double, or his ghost.

Later that sad and dismal afternoon, after everyone had gone, including the ladies of the church who had organized the meal, the four of them sat in the back pew of the church sanctuary. Major Joshua D'Angelo, the big Marine, was one of the four. He told Maggie, Rod and Larkin Richardson, about the charge Kiernan had put upon him the day before he died.

"I promised him I'd watch over you, Maggie. I will never intrude, except to save you, guide you, or protect you. If you call, I will come as soon as humanly possible. I am your brother man and you are my sister woman. From this day forward."

Joshua, her six-foot-nine Cajun angel, kept his promise from that day on.

*****

Through the curtain of tears, our vision wavers, blurring reflections of the ones who were taken away and have gone

108

on ahead of us. Though now in shadow, they remain as long as we remember them.

I can't even remember the sound of his voice calling my name, or singing his love songs to me. I no longer have tears for Kiernan. None.

The cats interrupted her sojourn down the back roads of memory, begging for attention. She sat on the loveseat with a cat on each side purring a duet in feline contentment.

Laura Blue, her mother-in-law, had died five years ago. She and Laura had never quite hit it off, but they were always polite for convention's sake. As for Emory Blue, Maggie and he got along very well. They talked on the phone at least once a month.

She yawned and stood up, dislodging the cats. They went pell-mell for the bed and hopped up on the far pillow.

Now that she had a home in Baysinger Cove, she should call Emory and maybe pay him a visit.

Tomorrow.

Sherrill M. Lewis

24

Grand Opening

THE WEATHER COOPERATED, more or less, for the Grand Opening celebration of Mariposa Crazy Cottage. At ten o'clock, the temperature was hovering at a bracing eighteen degrees under a grudging sun. The mayor strung a bright blue ribbon between the posts of the front porch at the top of the steps. Pictures were taken, the ribbon was cut, and Elda Carmichael made the shortest speech in her history as mayor. This made the three-minute ceremony itself the shortest one in the town's history, which earned the momentary gratitude of the shivering attendees. Within ten minutes, those same people were wandering around the shop, or in the kitchen sampling the cookies from the Stellar Bakery, the pastries from Sweet Things, and guzzling gallons of hot-spiced cider.

Many of the other merchants along Franklin Road dropped by to wish her well before heading back to their own shops. Larkin was answering questions while Pattysue did her best to wait on customers. Rod was busy ringing up sales.

Pattysue pulled Maggie aside. "I'm sorry, Maggie. People keep asking me about K-Kaleen, and I can't stand the pity in their eyes and their platitudes." She pulled a tissue out of her pocket and wiped her eyes.

110

"If you want to go home, go. We'll manage. When Autumn gets here, she can help just as easily. Or you can sneak upstairs, camp out in my sitting room with the cats, or take a nap. Your choice. But I'll keep my ears open for any news."

"I think I'll go home. In case the phone rings."

As soon as Pattysue left by way of the parlor door, Maggie went to the kitchen. She tied a fresh cheesecloth bundle filled with aromatic spices to the special hook attached to the side of one of the two big stainless steel kettles she had borrowed from Larkin. The delectable aroma of apple cider simmering on the stove filled the Cottage.

CJ was ladling hot cider out of the other kettle when he looked past her shoulder and broke out with a Texas-sized grin. She spun around to see what he was smiling about then ran straight for the kitchen door. "Joshua!"

"Sister woman!" Big as a mountain, six-foot-nine Joshua Dufrene D'Angelo, still Cajun-handsome at sixty, had both arms out to catch her. He lifted her up and kissed her good and proper before lowering her to the floor. Standing beside him, all six feet of Creole-gorgeous, Damia D'Angelo smiled, wrapped her arms around Maggie and kissed her cheek.

"I am so glad to see you both! *Merci beaucoup*! Thank you for coming!"

"Would not miss your big day, *chérie*," Damia replied, holding her at arm's length. "You are a-lookin' good, girl-friend. Happy, you?"

"Oh, yes, Damia, quite happy."

CJ was still grinning as he shook Joshua's hand. "Great to see you again, Joshua. But I haven't met your lady."

When Joshua first got the news from Maggie about the renewed romance with her high school sweetheart, he went to work doing what he did best. Unbeknownst to her at the time, Joshua had checked out the mature man. During one of CJ's periodic visits to his ranch in Texas, Joshua showed up. Over that three-day visit, both men learned what the other was all about. Joshua vetted CJ, and CJ gained a new and forever friend.

"We are thirty-five years married." He turned to his wife. "Damia, my dove, this is Miss Maggie's very special man: CJ Dubois."

CJ reached to shake her hand, but Damia was a hugger.

She released CJ then sniffed. "Be that hot spiced cider?"

"It's the way you taught me to make it, Damia. Help yourself. Do tell me you are in town long enough to be here for Thanksgiving, like always?" Maggie wanted to bounce up and down for joy at seeing these precious old friends. "Please say you are."

"*Boo*, ever since the day we met at Kiernan Blue's funeral, we've spent nearly every Thanksgiving holiday together. No reason to miss this one, is there?"

"Not a bit of it, dear friend. My folks hoped you would continue our little tradition."

"Different latitude, longitude, and altitude, but no change in attitude," Joshua sang in his deep base rumble.

It was from the love song Kiernan had written for Maggie for their first anniversary. Many years ago, long before she'd packed such things away, she had shown the score to Joshua. She wondered why he had pulled this out of his prodigious photographic memory banks, but he never did anything without a reason. She shivered like a goose had walked across her grave, and then realized with a start that the song no longer affected her in the way hearing it used to do.

Whatcha gonna do, Maggie Storm Blue?

Put you back in that cardboard casket where you belong. CJ's the love of my life now. It's time for me to mosey on down the road and leave you behind. Hmmm, in mysteries of old, the author would write: "Had she but known."

"What are you snickering about, Maggie?" Autumn and Chad Taylor interrupted her rampant thoughts. After hugs, Autumn set a fall-themed floral arrangement on the table before shooing Maggie out of the kitchen.

"Go on, mingle with your guests," Chad urged. "We'll take care of the food."

"Thanks. Autumn, I need you to help with customers, if you would. I sent Pattysue home. Too many questions and pitying eyes."

"I understand. Sure thing." She hung her coat in the hall closet before going in the shop.

Maisie and Terrance O'Reilly breezed in, each giving Maggie a quick hug and saying a blessing for much success. "Art at the Depot holiday gift gallery opens at noon, and our esteemed presence there is requested, me darlin'. Mustn't be a minute late. Do drop by and visit. Best place in Maine to buy your Christmas bits and bobbles."

Terrance raised his white bushy eyebrows and winked. His square-chiseled chin sported a fine beard and a big-hearted welcoming smile while his forehead was chasing his hairline goodbye. He was born in America, third generation of fine Irish stock. Many years in the service as an officer curbed some of the accent, but he never lost the blarney. To-day he was on his best behavior, but that wink said not for long.

Maisie glanced at her watch, smiled at Maggie, looked at her husband and announced, "Must toddle." She tucked her arm in her husband's and they toddled.

On a tall wooden lectern in the hall, Larkin had placed a guest book with a large sign reminding people to sign in. Maggie ran her finger down the page and was surprised to find Wayne Hardy's name. She found him returning to the parlor from the back porch.

"Housewarming gift." He jerked his thumb over his shoulder in the direction of the porch. "The other day, you mentioned wanting more bird feeders when my next shipment came in. I just beat you to it. I brought two, filled them, and hung them up for you, too." He held up the empty feed sack. "Just so you know, this mix has safflower seeds in it instead of sunflower seeds."

"That's so sweet of you, Wayne. Thank you ever so much. But what's the difference?"

"Squirrels don't like safflower, but the birds absolutely love it. Keeps those pesky squirrels from raiding your feeders and trashing them. We also carry sunflower seeds if you really want to feed the squirrels and chipmunks."

"I never knew that. And I suppose this specialty birdseed is only available at your store?" she asked in mock snootiness.

"Well, yeah! It's a recipe I made up special for our local birds. We bag the seeds in reusable cloth sacks. When you bring the bag in for a refill, you save money. Tony sewed up hundreds of sacks for us." For a moment the grief ravaging his three-decade-old face made him resemble the Ancient Mariner.

She touched his arm. "My heart and sympathies go out for your loss," she whispered. A trite phrase, but she couldn't think of anything else to say, more so since she only knew him business-wise.

"I wish our last words weren't so angry. Tony often exasperated me, but I loved him!" Wayne snatched a tissue from the box on the coffee table and swiped his eyes. "The poor boy thought I'd been unfaithful. He accused me of having an affair with the stock boy at the Mercantile."

A hateful word said, cannot be retracted. An angry deed cannot be undone. A rock thrown cannot be called back. A life taken away is gone forever.

Maggie wanted to steer the conversation around to Kaleen's disappearance but waited until Wayne was recovered from his small outburst.

He was way ahead of her. "Any news? Who would take off with a child?"

"Would *you*?" Maggie blurted it out before she thought, but Wayne didn't seem to take offense.

"Good heavens, no! I mean ... children as a collective are generally insufferably rude and insolent little people."

"Rather like some big people who consider themselves adults."

"Agreed. Some are disarmingly delightful little people, though." Wayne nodded. "I like Kaleen. That little girl is so sweet and polite. Pattysue Morgan has always been kind to us." He shuddered. "Oh my! I just realized Kaleen is Robert

Morgan's daughter!"

Maggie waited, hoping Wayne would elaborate. He didn't disappoint her.

"I was over at the Mercantile late one night. Morgan was drunk, as usual. He jerked me out of the car, called me filthy names, and started beating the stuffing out of me. I thought, silly me, I'd left that sort of vicious prejudice behind in Chicago. Lucky for me, a nice big handsome deputy came by and rescued me." He looked wistful. "But the deputy was straight." His sigh came all the way up from his shoes. He gave Maggie a one-armed hug, surprising her, before he departed.

Would Wayne have taken Kaleen as belated revenge for that beating? Oh, come on, that's too far-fetched even for a dime-store mystery novel! I need to get back to my customers for a reality check.

The Quilt Society members did not disappoint Maggie either. Even if they were not embellishers, they came out of curiosity. Later they'd tell their friends. Maggie relied on the six degrees of separation theory, whereby the word about her shop would spread exponentially.

Larkin's CQ Circle ladies came out in full force and shopped. Some spent a little, some spent a lot. Liberty Birdwell, new to the world of crazy quilts, bought a lot. She was very excited about the upcoming classes and was overjoyed when she was told she had earned a fifteen-percent discount on her first class.

Several more discount certificates were awarded that afternoon. Larkin was in charge of gathering information from the qualifying customers. She had each awardee fill out a class questionnaire. Then Larkin signed and dated the form along with a note of the discount percentage earned. "Classes will start up in January," she told each of them. "Something pleasant to look forward to after the holiday letdown."

25

A Day of Rest

PEOPLE MILLED AROUND THE FRONT HALL for coffee and doughnuts, as well as to catch up on the latest news in the twenty minutes between Sunday school and the church service. In between snippets of conversations about whose grandchildren were or were not coming for the big turkey day event, there was an undercurrent of unease about young Kaleen's disappearance right after Tony Leblanc's murder. There had to be a connection between the two events, didn't there—but what, was the common question. Beyond casual, sometimes heated, speculation, no one seemed to know anything specific that Maggie could take back to the sheriff.

A little sparrow of a woman dressed in every color of the rainbow toddled up to Maggie and CJ. Berry-bright eyes peered out of a dark dried-apple-doll face. Her fine white hair looked like fairy feathers floating around her head. She leaned on a hickory knot cane, its whorls and knobs an echo of the woman's body it supported.

A brown-skinned hand, knotty and crab-clawed with arthritis, reached out. Maggie held the woman's small hand with care, afraid of hurting her. It had the texture of fine parchment paper overlaying bird bones.

When she spoke, in direct contradiction to her appearance, her voice was gentle and strong. "I like to talk about my Jesus," she said. "Do you know Him?"

"Yes, sweet lady, I truly do."

"What about you, young man?" Bright brown eyes peered way up at CJ.

CJ chuckled. "Yes, ma'am, I do."

Maggie was enchanted. "What is your name?"

"Why, I am Time herself, child." Her laugh sounded like a waterfall over granite pebbles. "Sylvia Rosalie L'Heure."

Maggie smiled at the old woman's play on words. "Of course!"

"Doesn't *'heure'* mean 'hour'? French class was too many years ago," CJ said, taking the old woman's hand in his. He leaned down and kissed her cheek.

Sylvia giggled. "Thank you. I'm glad you both caught the pun." Sparrow-quick she turned to join the tide of people walking toward the sanctuary. "Walk with me."

Maggie and CJ went in, with Sylvia bobbing along on her cane between them.

"I've been a member of Graceline Baptist Church since the doors first opened twenty-five years ago. My great-grandmother was a slave down in Georgia. My mama taught me to sing and to choose my own special quiet ministry. Different from other folks' choices, you hear?"

"We hear you, ma'am. What's your specialty?" CJ asked when she stopped in mid-stride to look up at him again.

"You're a Texas boy, aren't you?"

"Was for a spell, but I'm back home now."

"Good for you. Well, now, son, my ministry is to sit in the front pew right smack-dab in the middle to free up a back row seat. Most people avoid it. They'd rather be in the anonymous row way back there. Front row's always the best seat in the house. You folks sit in the third row on the gospel side, don't you?" She was traveling at a good pace for a very elderly lady with a cane.

Though Sylvia was a long-time member of this church, her Episcopalian roots were showing when she mentioned the gospel side of the church. When facing the pulpit, it was the left side of the church. The epistle was at the right-hand side of the pulpit.

Maggie had long ceased to be amazed at how many people knew who she was, while she was still learning her way around town. Birdie Mandrell's news-vine was light-years faster than even the Internet to get the scuttlebutt scattered. Birdie's news spread the scandalous while the *Baywater County Chronicle* skirted the libelous.

*****

"Freaky weather," Maggie commented after lunch. "It's fifty degrees now. Whatever happened to buckets of snow already on the ground by this late in November? Or is my memory faulty?"

"Global warming gets the blame." Larkin wiped the sink and laid the dishcloth across the divider. "Won't last, I'm afraid. There's a cold front blowing our way."

"Snow is my favorite weather." Maggie was caught up in the romance of sitting by a cozy fire with hot chocolate and a classic cozy mystery. It would be even better if she were nestled up beside that same fire with CJ. "Quiet, soft, brilliant, serene flakes …" Then rude reality kicked in. "At least until it turns vicious and noisy, exchanging softness for wind-blown hard ice crystals."

Maggie finished putting the luncheon dishes in the dish-washer before she and Larkin adjourned to the Lake Room at Eagles' Rest. Now that she was settled in Baysinger Cove, they had established a tradition of gathering at her folks' home for lunch after church.

"What did you end up doing with Aunt June's estate?" Maggie chose one of the two club chairs. June Scoular was Rod's older sister. He had out-lived all three of his siblings.

Rod leaned back in his recliner. "June disowned her son Victor. She set it up so that the three girls, her nieces, would inherit. The estate was never to pass down to their children, but over to me to do with as I saw fit, if for whatever reason they couldn't inherit. All three of your sisters, er, cousins, had a hand in her death. Since a murderer cannot profit from the deed, I inherited. Also as executor it was left up to me, so I donated the balance after June's funeral expenses to the animal shelter." He chuckled and raised the footrest.

"Is that some kind of renegade justice?" CJ asked.

"Ayuh, you might say that. She had no love for cats or dogs. Neither did she understand the plight of the homeless. When her house sells, that money will go to the homeless shelter. Yes, ironic justice."

Maggie agreed that these were both very worthwhile causes. "I've seen people on the sidewalk with cardboard signs seeking a donation or asking for work. My heart wants to help, but I am wary to trust. One day I watched a man leave his post, walk through the parking lot and drive away in an upscale late-model car. Therein is my dilemma. Either he was faking the need, or that car was all he had left to claim as his own. In most big cities, I've seen homeless people sleeping in cardboard boxes under bridges, or worse."

"Are you wondering how people get that way?" CJ asked. "Mostly circumstances and consequences."

"When it comes close to home, then it has more meaning," Larkin said.

"Quite true. Shortly before I left Tucson, a neighbor's sixteen-year-old daughter by a previous marriage got in a horrendous fight with her stepfather. She was pregnant, and he kicked her out. She moved in with her boyfriend and had the baby a few months later. The misguided, immature dad couldn't stand the baby's fussing so he left. She had no job, no money, and no choice. She contacted her mother, who refused to help, blaming her husband, the step-dad. After a while, even her friends living in small apartments couldn't take on two houseguests for more than a week. No room, and not much money for extra groceries, stretched the friendships. She soon ran out of friends. The two of them lived on the street for several months."

"I hope this sad story has a happy ending." Larkin pulled a lace-edged hanky out of her pocket, lifted her glasses and wiped her eyes. She had a small wooden chest full of dainty hankies. Some were her mother's, and others were gifts from a very young Maggie.

"She finally mustered up enough courage to call her father. He paid for her and the baby to fly from Tucson to Oklahoma City. He raised the roof over the garage and converted the dusty crawl space into a sunny apartment for them.

Her dad's new wife is delighted with the little boy and is a willing babysitter. The girl got a job at a fast-food chicken place. It's a start in the right direction."

"She's very lucky her father helped her out and his wife is so supportive." CJ said. "Doesn't always happen that way."

"Her dad was one of my clients in Oklahoma City. That's just the kind of people they are."

"So, why didn't she call him sooner?" Rod asked.

"Who knows? Pride, maybe. Scared, most likely." Maggie pushed her glasses up on her nose. "At least this story did have a happy ending, Larkin."

"How's Pattysue doing?" Larkin asked. "I hope she has a happy ending to her story, too. She's staying busy but she's running on autopilot. Seeing those dark shadows under her eyes, I just know she's not sleeping well."

"She knows she can't do much about it except pray," Maggie said. "And wait."

"It's the waiting, and not knowing, that's the hardest part," CJ said. "Praying is easy. Walker questioned some of Pattysue's neighbors about seeing any strangers in the area. There was a door-to-door salesman selling magazine subscriptions the same afternoon Kaleen disappeared. Another neighbor noticed there was also a green pickup truck that was moving awfully slow up the road. And a red Jeep."

"That sounds ominous," Rod said.

"Quite true. Yesterday during a lull at the Cottage, Pattysue called Charlotte's cell phone. The signal was weak, due to another storm, according to her mother-in-law," Maggie said. "There seems to be an inordinate amount of storm activity wherever Charlotte is. Too much."

"I'll check online for the weather in the area. If I see anything significant, I'll call Walker," CJ said.

"Did Pattysue say anything else?" Larkin asked.

"She said she thought she heard a child's voice in the background. When she questioned it, Charlotte told her it was only the TV. After she disconnected, Pattysue started crying again. She didn't want to go home, so I let her stay."

"It was cold yesterday, but there was no major storm anywhere in Baywater County or the surrounding counties," CJ said. "Up north usually gets storms before we do. Walker contacted the Camden police to check on the Morgan's' house this morning. The housekeeper said Charlotte and Paul were out shopping or something. She hasn't seen Kaleen, but the housekeeper is only there one day a week."

"Maybe Charlotte isn't in Camden but somewhere else. Is it possible for the sheriff to pinpoint where that cell phone is, like GPS tracking?" Maggie asked, a card-carrying technologically challenged inhabitant of the twenty-first century.

"If it's turned on, it's possible," Rod answered, technology being his bailiwick. "I'll call Walker, just in case he hasn't talked to Pattysue since you saw her yesterday. Maggie, didn't you say that Cooper disappeared the same day Kaleen was taken?"

"Quite right, he did."

"Could he have taken her?" Rod asked.

"He'd have let Pattysue know by now, at least we hope he would," Larkin said. She was looking through a new art quilting magazine.

"Is it possible that Charlotte has Kaleen?" Maggie asked.

"She's threatened to sue for custody of the child. But either one of them would have the foresight to pack a little suitcase."

"Charlotte would be either stupid or crazy to do it," Rod said. "Kidnapping is a major offense with jail time attached. It'd make more sense for her to go the legal route."

"No one ever said criminals were overly gifted in the smarts department. Charlotte switches from playing the full poor me/martyr card to the guilt trip she tries to lay on Pattysue. I am surprised that she's not all a-dither about Kaleen's absence, she dotes on the child so much." Maggie rotated her neck and shrugged her shoulders to relieve a crick that had been annoying her.

CJ sat on the arm of her club chair, turned her sideways and began to massage her shoulders. "I wonder, too. Maybe she's staying calm so she won't upset Pattysue."

Maggie felt like purring as she leaned back against CJ's strong hands.

"Staying calm simply for her daughter-in-law's sake does not fit that woman's frame of reference," Larkin said with asperity.

"Thank you, CJ. That felt wonderful."

Rod got up to answer the phone. He returned to his recliner a few minutes later. "The sheriff is no closer to solving Tony's murder, but he does have two clues he's keeping close to the vest. He'll talk with you later about one of them, Maggie. And I'll say no more because I don't know any more."

Maggie sighed, knowing it was futile to badger her father for more information, and changed the subject. "What do

Pattysue's parents think?"

"They aren't quite as militant about their daughter's choice of a husband. Last time I talked to Audra, she said they like Cooper Larradeau and Roy Grayson both. As long as Pattysue is happy, they are, too," Larkin said.

"Would they have taken Kaleen to keep the child out of Charlotte Morgan's clutches?" Maggie asked, remembering the snatch of conversation overheard at the Sawmill last week.

"I sincerely doubt it, my dear," Rod said, folding the paper and dropping it in the basket beside his chair.

"Oh, well. Since we've got a houseful here for Thanksgiving, I'm closing the Cottage at two on Wednesday. I'll make the pumpkin, pecan, and harvest apple pies. Damia has offered to help me, which is a real treat. Anything else you want me to make?" Maggie asked, happy to be on a more-fun topic.

"Can I be your taste-tester?" CJ asked with a cheeky grin that set Maggie's heart pitter-pattering. He made himself comfortable in the companion club chair. "I'll bring a spiral cut ham."

They discussed the guest list and the who's-bringing-what menu until Larkin's legal pad was filled. She laid her pen down on the pad. "Well, that's done. The turkey is thawing in a pan of cold water in the utility room sink. Rod secured the cover so Siam can't get at it."

Siam jumped up in Larkin's lap and batted the pen onto the floor. He hopped down and in short order subdued the evil writing stick. He stood up and took one of those luxurious limb-by-limb stretches that only cats can do.

"I'll keep my fur-kids upstairs while I'm cooking, though I don't think they like pies."

"Cats like pumpkin, didn't you know?" CJ reached down to scratch Sheba's ears. She leaned against his legs with a look of canine bliss on her sweet furry face.

"No kidding? Then they *will* be banned from my kitchen. But you won't be, CJ."

"I'm real good at peeling apples."

Maggie smiled and returned her attention to Larkin. "How did your Sewing Circle gals do Friday night? I was with Pattysue quite a while, then I flat out forgot."

"Being the Friday before Thanksgiving, not many showed up. In December we'll have our annual party. Nearly everyone comes to that one. Beginning in January, what do you think about hosting the Circle at your shop?" Larkin suggested. "We could announce it at the party."

"Fine by me. Maybe I wouldn't forget to come if y'all were meeting at the Cottage!"

Larkin laughed and reminded Maggie that it would also help to drive business. "The ramp and the shallow steps on the side porch will help those with mobility issues to attend, like Artesia Lovington." Artesia had wanted to be part of Larkin's crazy quilt circle but she had difficulty climbing stairs.

Maggie fully agreed. Not only for convenience and to boost business, Larkin was closing in fast on her eighth decade. Although her mother was still spry, Maggie had noticed that Larkin was dropping some of her activities, and saying "no" much more often.

Because her most recent job before moving to Maine was

in copywriting, Maggie loved to skim through the list of home-for-sale ads. She plucked the Sunday paper out of the basket beside her father's chair and settled back in her chair.

"Oh, how funny! Listen to this: 'Great neighborhood with new carpet.' That rug must have cost a bundle! How about this one? 'Newly remodeled business people and free children.' Not many takers, I'll bet."

"That's scary for any number of reasons," CJ remarked, shaking his head.

"Someone should send them an envelope full of commas," Larkin said. "With instructions to use the punctuation more liberally."

Maggie giggled. "Here's another doozy. 'Huge covered patio plumbed for spa and mountain and sunset views.' It must be a pretty crowded patio or a highly specialized plumbing job."

"I'd like to meet the plumber that pulled off that job," Rod said, laughing. "Plumb a mountain? Maybe. A sunset?"

26

Early Bird

JUST SHY OF THE BLUE HOUR Monday morning, Maggie's bedside phone rang. Not a good way to start off her day. The sun was about to discard the bedcovers of night and stretch up toward the horizon. She groped for the phone, disobliging the cats. After mumbling some semblance of a greeting, she heard a faint noise right before the caller began talking.

"Your Windows operating system needs an upgrade." The man sounded like he was juggling marbles in his mouth. "For only $299 we can fix this—"

Though very groggy from being jerked out of a sound sleep, she still caught the intended scam. "Are you serious?" she interrupted, sitting up and rubbing her eyes.

"Yes. Hurry or your system will crash in the next hour!"

Really? "No, it won't."

"Fifty-eight minutes."

Surely not. "Listen, *mister*, Macs don't have that problem," she said, wondering why she was even talking to this person. *I need coffee, now.*

"Fifty-five! You must upgrade immediately! I need your credit card—"

She hung up on him, no longer willing to spare a few more minutes of peace for whomever he called next.

"Sheesh." Any hope of going back to sleep was not in her immediate future. "C'mon, kids. Might as well get up." As soon as she slid out of bed, two fur kids crawled under the blankets, taking over her vacated warm spot. "Lazy bones."

The phone rang again, but there was no one there. "Probably a wrong number."

Yawns and stretches punctuated her usual grace with uncharacteristic and awkward motions until she could get the early morning kinks out. She wasn't as limber as she used to be now that she was past the half-century mark. Much of her exercise over the years came from dancing three or four nights a week. How long *had* it been? A month? Surely not—well, maybe. She made a mental note to suggest to CJ a two-steppin' night out very soon.

Waiting in the kitchen while the coffeepot took forever to dribble out the java-jump-jiving morning elixir, she thought about that ridiculous phone call. The voice reminded her of an old James Cagney gangster film from the nineteen-thirties, and sounded just like him. "Come on, coffee, brew!"

Other than listening to disjointed chatter and asking a few questions as she met people while running errands or having idle conversation with her customers, she wasn't doing much sleuthing or consulting with the sheriff this time. When her customers were talking about the murder or the kidnapping among themselves or with her, might the murderer also be in the shop, listening?

While a load of laundry was going, she straightened up her living quarters, and made a mental note to set the automatic brew cycle on the coffeepot before going to bed tonight.

27

Shop and Gossip

ART AT THE DEPOT HAD OPENED its Holiday Gift Gallery the same day that Maggie had the Grand Opening of her shop. Knowing how crazy the stores would be on the day after Thanksgiving, Maggie decided that going shopping this morning held far more appeal than doing paperwork.

Truth be told, with the excellent inventory-tracking system Rod had created, sales totals were run daily and a weekly report was printed on Saturdays—bless his Yankee buttons—so there wasn't much left for her to do today. "Shopping, it is!"

A quick look at the inventory report assured her that no stock needed to be reordered this week with the one exception of the best-selling needle threader. She went online, placed the order then shut her computer down. To ensure that the cats' deep-seated curiosity wouldn't create cyber-havoc, she turned off the keyboard and the mouse then tucked both in the desk's middle drawer.

*****

Wandering around what once was the train station's elegant waiting room, she marveled at the creativity of the various artists. They had retained the old-time charm while making the large room appealing to today's shoppers with the various crafts displayed on glass shelving units.

Though she had purchased Maisie's painting for both of her parents last week, she wanted to find something nice for each of them. Looking through the multi-colored scarves hanging on a waterfall rack, she found a hand-dyed, cut-velvet scarf in shades of deep teal blue that would be perfect for Larkin.

She petted a rabbit-fur-lined leather vest created by the same artist who made the slippers Rod had given her for her birthday. Lest the anti-fur brigade were to rear up in abject horror, all hangtags stated that the artist raised rabbits for food and used the fur to enhance his leather garments. The non-edible portions were tossed out for the eagles residing on Old Man Mountain. Nothing was wasted.

Fur-lined leather jackets were on the same circular garment rack. A black jacket for CJ and a brown vest for Rod went to the front desk for safekeeping since they wouldn't fit in the gallery's wicker shopping basket.

The Depot was a busy place this afternoon. She tuned out conversations as so much extraneous white noise until she heard a woman mention Wayne Hardy's name.

"I think Wayne must've killed Tony. Stands to reason if Tony—"

"Why d'you think that," the second woman interrupted. "That idiot …" An announcement over the speaker canceled out the name. "… I'm telling you … a nutcase. Ought to be put away … it's for his own good. Wilma said Wayne had a nasty run-in with him. Remember?"

"When was that?"

"Don't rightly recall. A while back."

A man bundled up in a quilted camouflage jacket joined the women. "I heard there was a shoving match ... He thought Tony was dissing him ..."

Other people talking and laughing overrode the man's words, much to Maggie's annoyance.

"Turn a shove into murder? Ain't likely," the first woman said as she moved away. "Say, you still riding that black monster, even in this cold weather?"

"Which one? The horse or the Harley?"

After two hours of happy browsing, she had checked off the most important people on her Christmas gift list.

She strolled along the gallery wall where Mike Richaud's stunning photographs were showcased. The one with a riot of butterflies ascending was no longer there. Oh, well. Can't dither in an art gallery. Items are one of a kind and, if you waited too long, you could well lose out.

Satisfied with what she had chosen for gifts, she walked to the cash desk. Several people were in line ahead of her, chatting away, adding more leaves to Birdie's news-vine.

The woman talking the most had salon-perfect auburn hair. "Pattysue's mother-in-law is a harridan. Bet she gets custody of the little girl before she's done."

"Not hardly," her companion in a Nordic sweater retorted. "Pattysue's a fighter. It'll take more'n Charlotte's chutzpah to pull that off. Did you see that Amber Alert on TV last night?"

"Yeah I did. That's so scary! You never know what's going on. The poor child, if she's still alive, I can't imagine how terrified she must be," the third woman said, shaking her head.

Maggie recognized Birdie Mandrell, right in the middle of a salacious gossip fest.

"But if Charlotte took Kaleen … wouldn't that sway the judge?" Mrs. Perfect asked.

Birdie nodded. "It might. But the accident happened a long time ago."

"Evil casts a long shadow," Mrs. Perfect announced.

"Her parents adore that little sweetheart. They'd put up a fight, too," Mrs. Sweater said with spirit.

Birdie brightened as she headed down another juicy gossip trail. "Who do you think she'll marry?"

28

D'Artagnan Arrives

MAGGIE WAS REPLACING THE LINER in the kitchen wastebasket when her front doorbell rang. She opened the front door to find CJ standing there. "Why didn't you park in the garage?"

CJ nodded to his right. Sitting beside him was a handsome tan and black German shepherd. His pointy ears were on alert and his gaze on Maggie. CJ motioned and said, "Dart, come." The proud dog stood up. "Dart, meet Maggie."

Dart walked up to Maggie and sat down.

"Dart, say hello."

The dog woofed once then put up a paw. At a nod from CJ, Maggie reached down to shake. "Oh, you're a gorgeous puppy," she cooed. Dart's tongue hung out giving her a goofy grin while his furry tail swept the porch floor.

The brisk wind made the ragged clouds look like laundry waving on a clothesline. Her teeth began to chatter. "It's c-cold out here." She chafed her crossed arms. "Could we continue this inside?"

CJ looked at the outside thermometer. "It's forty-five degrees, downright balmy."

"To me it's not."

CJ chuckled and led the dog inside. He pulled two bowls

out of the bag he'd brought in. He filled one bowl with water and set both bowls in the corner beside the antique hutch. Dart sniffed the empty bowl then slurped up most of the water before parking beside CJ's chair. "I've got a bag of dog food out in the car. I'll bring it in later."

"How did you get him? And why bring him here?" She had a sneaking suspicion when CJ mentioned dog food that her fur family was to increase by one.

"By the long way around the barn. Dart was mustered out early because of a serious leg injury. Joshua asked Walker to find a retired K-9 dog. Walker called a police associate of his and found out Dart was up for adoption. Joshua asked me to bring Dart to you."

"Interesting, that. Did he happen to say why?" Joshua didn't always reveal his reasons. She had learned early on to trust him.

"Why he didn't bring the dog to you himself?" CJ asked.

"That, too. But why bring me a dog at all?"

"He's been out of town doing some research, he told me. Why? Just that you will need him."

"Oh." She never questioned Joshua's reasons because they were always sound ones. Sometimes his actions were spooky in a preternatural sense. Not that he could see the future, but he had a phenomenal sense of what was going on around Maggie. Though he stayed in touch, he did not, as a rule, interfere with her life. However, over the span of their many-decade-long friendship, several times he had rescued her from consequences of her own folly.

Her cell phone rang its distinctive chime. "Hello, Joshua!"

"How're you doing with Dart, *boo*?"

"Dart just arrived. Thank you! He's gorgeous, and I love him already. We're going to introduce him to the cats in a bit."

"Do not go anywhere without him. Promise me. He'll be company, but more to the point, he will constantly protect you."

"I promise. Why do you feel I need constant protection?"

"I don't like your anonymous flower deliveries, *chérie*. Your last one was far more worrisome than the others, from what you told me about the symbolism. I've been looking around a bit."

"And?"

"Early days, yet, *boo*." Joshua cleared his throat. "Have you noticed any pattern to the timing of the deliveries?"

"I'd have to look in my journal to answer that precisely, Joshua. The single commonality is these have only occurred when I have been here in Baysinger Cove. Never when I lived out of state."

"Very interesting. Later, my sister woman. I love you."

"I love you, too, brother man." With a happy smile she disconnected the call before repeating the gist of the conversation to CJ.

"Joshua's on the trail of something." He reached down to scratch Dart's ears.

"Why's he called 'Dart'?"

"It's an abbreviation. He was named for the fourth Musketeer. His full name is D'Artagnan Gold Shield. His litter mates were named for the other three."

"Oh, how funny. How is he around civilians and cats?"

"No problem. Police dogs are trained to be stable around all animals and people. He will only attack when told to do so, unless you're in danger. When you want him to do something very specific, always say his name before the command. You noticed when I said *attack* like I just did, he didn't respond to the word. Say his name plus that 'a' word, and someone's day just went from bad to worse. He's incredibly intelligent." CJ paused. "Are you okay with another addition to our fur-kid family?"

I knew it! Maggie thought for a moment before agreeing. "No telling if the cats' background included dogs in the house. Regardless, I'm happy to include him. He may be good around cats, but I wonder how the cats are going to react to him?"

"We are about to find out." CJ pointed at the entrance to the parlor.

Tuffy and Rusty, like mismatched bookends, sat side-by-side in the doorway. Ears forward, eyes wide, and tails a-twitching, they stared at the dog. In chorus, they both growled once.

The dog looked up at CJ for direction.

"Dart, friends." CJ pointed to the cats.

Dart padded toward the doorway. He stopped near Maggie's chair when the cats arched their backs. He slid down on his belly with his tail swishing back and forth across the hardwood floor. The cats glanced up at Maggie before creeping forward. Dart sat up and leaned down to meet the advancing cats.

Dart sneezed, sending both cats scurrying backward. Recovering their innate sense of curiosity, they advanced on the dog.

"Dart, be nice," Maggie said, surprising herself by taking over the command.

Dart extended a paw first to Tuffy, who touched the dog's paw with his. Rusty, though the larger of the two cats, was more cautious. After a moment he also extended his furry paw. The cats sniffed noses with the dog.

"Good boys!" Maggie praised her fur-children.

"I think they've made peace."

"Quite so. Now, what was that comment about increasing *our* family? And we're not even married yet!" Maggie quipped. "Anyway, three is enough."

29

Fix-Its

"WE CAN FIX THAT," CJ OFFERED.

Dart laid his head in her lap. "Fix what?" Maggie petted the dog's head and ears. "You're so handsome." She leaned forward and dropped a soft kiss on the sleek canine head.

"Thank you."

Maggie looked up at CJ's broad grin and returned his smile. "You are *both* handsome."

"We haven't done our duet yet. Will you marry me?"

"You mean at the Rusty Anchor? No, we ... *What*?"

"Marry me."

"Oh. Well. Oh, my!"

Dart left Maggie and walked over to his water bowl for a loud, slurping drink.

"Well?" CJ's right eyebrow cocked skyward.

"I've been thinking about it, ever since we first became reacquainted. Last year, you intimated as much." Maggie twirled a lock of grey-threaded, black hair around her fingers.

"I've asked you before."

"True. But I knew you would ask me again, eventually." She stood up and walked toward him.

"Hey, *querida*, I'm still asking."

"Not to worry, dear heart. I shan't marry anyone else. So, you may ask me again, anytime." She sat down in his lap and kissed him.

*****

Maggie's cell cheeped. "Hi, Pattysue."

"Charlotte was just here, Maggie. We talked about K-Kaleen's disappearance. She sounded sincere about being concerned, told me Kaleen's probably just fine and no one would hurt her precious baby. Asked me if there'd been a ransom note yet. There hasn't been. But something's off."

Charlotte should know that child predators don't much care about the well-being of their victims, so why isn't she panicking—unless she's the kidnapper! But predators would not bother to pack a suitcase. "Off how?"

"Charlotte seemed distracted. She's not as upset as I would expect her to be when her only grandchild is missing. She's my daughter, and I'm scared, worried, and miserable." Pattysue paused. "The Amber Alert on TV hasn't brought any leads, either. The sheriff says a search party won't do any good. The dogs only traced Kaleen from Mrs. Sanger's driveway to the edge of the road. Someone picked her up … and … oh, my poor baby!"

"Oh, my friend, remember, the prayer warriors at church have sent out a prayer chain. Gotcha covered, Pattysue."

"It's all in God's hands, I know, but … " Pattysue trailed off, tears clogging her words.

"Keep us in the loop. We'll help any way we can." Maggie was close to crying, too.

Pattysue snuffled and blew her nose. "I w-will. Thanks, Maggie."

30

The Happy Bookworm

"**LET'S GO VISIT HAROLD.** He needs cheering up, and I'd like him to meet our new little friend."

CJ clipped the lead to Dart's collar and handed the leash to her. "Little? He weighs in at seventy-five pounds, easy."

Maggie reiterated the gist of Pattysue's call while they crossed the street. "Kaleen wasn't with Charlotte. Could she have been at home with Paul?"

"Maybe. Do you think Paul had anything to do with his granddaughter's disappearance?"

"I've never met him, so I can't say. Pattysue always speaks favorably about him. It's her mother-in-law she butts heads with, sort of like the way I got along with my mother-in-law."

"I like your parents, a lot. You know you won't have to worry about in-law issues with me."

When CJ was ten years old, he saw his stepfather shoot his mother. The man was later executed.

"What happened to your birth father?"

"He was killed in a car accident when I was five. I don't remember him much, except for small bits."

Dart trotted at her side just like he'd always been there.

Between the front door squeaking and the vintage sleigh

bells jingling, there was no way to surprise Harold. He rushed out from behind his desk to greet them. "Hello, hello! Two frequent shoppers and a guest!"

"Hi, Harold. Hello, Chester," Maggie said, hooking her finger around a bar of his cage.

The pet crow danced around, squawking. *"Hello, gorgeous!"*

Dart cocked his head at the noisy bird saying people words. Chester stuck his glossy black head through the bars and looked down at Dart. *"Who's that?"*

Maggie introduced the dog to the bookseller and his pet bird.

Harold beamed. "Oh, he's a handsome fellow and so personable. He looks very smart, too. You can see it in his eyes."

"That he is." Maggie felt the pride of being a new parent. *Out of wedlock, yet!* She felt the heat of a blush watching CJ's grin as if he could read her thoughts. Dart stuck his cold nose in the palm of her hand, bringing her with a jolt back to earth.

CJ asked Harold, "How are you holding up? Everything here okay?"

"Oh, I've been doing as well as can be expected. Business has picked up some. Whether it's the holiday season or simply ghouls hoping to see bloodstains, I don't know."

"Ghouls!"

Dart looked at the bird again but kept his distance. Maggie reached down and petted the dog, hoping to reassure him. *Cats, other dogs, people, Dart's fine with them all. Perhaps birds like Chester are outside his frame of reference.*

"What's today's word?" she asked. Every week, Harold unearthed an old or obscure word for his Word of the Day contest. The first person to define it won a ten-percent discount on one book. Usually she or Larkin won, whoever got to the bookstore first.

Harold looked smug. "Caitiff."

"Oh, that's way too easy! A caitiff is a mean, bad person."

"Like the person who murdered Tony Leblanc," CJ suggested.

"You surely must have heard the shot, Harold," Maggie said.

"Yes ... I heard it."

"So, didn't you see who shot him? He couldn't have made it to the front door that fast," she persisted.

"Well, no, on both counts. Well, I was ...well, I was indisposed at the time."

A gentleman out of another century, Harold was, but Maggie caught the euphemism. "Oh!"

"When I got to the front, Wayne was holding Tony's head in his lap and sobbing his heart out. I called emergency."

"Where was Wayne before Tony was shot?" CJ asked.

"He was over by that small bookcase where I have the cookbooks. From there you can't see the door or the area where Tony was. Wayne said the shot startled him. He grabbed the bookcase, and it fell over. By the time he unburied himself from under all those books, it was too late to see anyone or do anything." Harold pulled a snow-white handkerchief out of his jacket pocket, removed his glasses and wiped his face.

"Now, I've got a word for you, Harold," Maggie said, changing the subject. "Colligation."

"Is that something to do with collecting?" He replaced his handkerchief in his pocket and put his glasses on his nose.

"Quite so. It's the orderly bringing together of isolated facts that lead to truth."

"So far," CJ said, "the facts have been anything but orderly." He reached for the dog's leash. "Tony's murder, Kaleen's disappearance, the Lone Ranger, and licorice."

31

Love, Always

LATER THAT EVENING MAGGIE pulled the decorative box that held her journals out of the small closet. She didn't write every day; sometimes she only gave a brief overview of the previous week's activities. A standard-format, bound book could last from three to five years. She began journaling right before her marriage to Kiernan.

She had drawn little symbols in the margins to help identify special events. Double rings were beside their wedding date. A stylized tree was drawn for their first Christmas. Skipping the pages for March and April of 1972 edged with black ink, she saw a small vase with a single rose drawn beside June seventh that same year.

Kiernan died in Viet Nam from sniper fire in late March. He was buried on the first day of April.

Every year on June seventh a red rose in a small bud vase was delivered to her door with a pretty florist's card that said: *Love, Always*. She supposed Kiernan must have set up the continuing anniversary rose deliveries with his mother. Laura would have kept track of where Maggie was, only to honor her son's wish, not out of any great love for her daughter-in-law. In spite of Maggie's frequent moves, annual Christmas cards kept them in contact with one another.

Sherrill M. Lewis

Laura died five years ago, but the roses kept coming. Had her father-in-law Emory Blue continued the legacy?

That still did not answer the question about the other roses delivered when she least expected them and tossed without any care as to where they landed on the porch. Single roses, each bouquet proclaiming a secret message unless one knew the Victorian language of flowers like she and Kiernan did.

She put the box back in the closet then sat down to update her current journal. She set this journal on the lower shelf of the antique smoking stand beside her chair.

The two cats nudged her. Dart put one paw on her knee and whimpered.

"Okay, gang, message received. I'm done. Bedtime!"

32

Busy, Busier

VERY EARLY TUESDAY MORNING, Dotty Thystleberry tapped on the front door. She was carrying a large cloth shopping bag. "This is for you," she said once they were in the kitchen. Looking anxious, she handed the bag to Maggie.

Taking a quick peek, Maggie first saw a riot of rainbow colors. She pulled out an old-fashioned granny-square afghan, crocheted in every color that she liked. Each square was bordered in the traditional black yarn. "You made this for me?" Maggie asked as she clutched the softness to her cheek. "It's gorgeous."

Dotty's face glowed with pleasure at Maggie's reaction. "Yes, for you." Then she grew pensive. "I'm sorry I was mean to you ... before. Playing naughty tricks on you wasn't nice."

Ain't that the truth! Maggie remembered the non-harmful but very annoying herbal messages and odd lots of mischief Dotty had plagued them with during the cottage remodel last month. Dotty had believed that the cottage was still hers, though she'd lost it several years ago for non-payment of taxes. She hadn't liked a stranger in "her" home, much less one making major changes. Maggie's kindness won the old woman over, which was the beginning of a tenuous friendship.

"I forgave you, remember?"

"I remember." Dotty nodded. "You said you like bright colors. I thought the afghan might look pretty in the other room."

"Oh, it will. Thank you so very much." Maggie draped the lap-robe-sized treasure over the back of the burgundy-upholstered loveseat in the parlor, where it looked very much at home. "Pretty and perfect."

*****

Maggie was replenishing stock when a man and a woman opened the door, bringing a blast of cold air in with them. Dart looked up from his vigil in the kitchen doorway, alert but non-aggressive.

The woman unbuttoned her coat and looked around the shop. She was short, small boned, and delicate. Her faded blonde French braid went halfway down her back.

The man was about Maggie's height of five-nine. With a round face, dark brown eyes, and a full beard framing a small mouth with a slight overbite, he looked like a chubby elf, minus the pointy ears. It was next to impossible not to like him. He went to sit in one of the visitor's chairs by the front window near the cutting table.

"May I help you?"

"You don't remember me, do you, Maggie?"

That question always made her uneasy. She was glad she wasn't alone in the shop. Larkin was in the classroom packaging patterns, and CJ was camped in the parlor, reading.

"No, you have the advantage."

"Debbie Dinsmore, and that's my husband David."

David was balancing the wooden chair on its back legs, whistling. Maggie feared for the longevity of the chair's spindly legs. She vowed to exchange those pretty chairs for metal folding ones as soon as these people departed.

Maggie still had no clue, and the poker-player she wasn't must have alerted Debbie to be more forthcoming with information.

"It's been a long time! No wonder you don't recognize me. We're cousins, you and me. I was Deborah Ghoulson. You remember my sisters, Susie and Joanie? We all live over in North Wainwright now."

"Do you, now. The last time I saw you, you were in pig-tails and I didn't wear glasses."

"You haven't changed much. Your hair's still mostly black, and your eyes are that distinctive green."

"Thank you." *She's a cousin by marriage, not by blood, though Debbie may not know the details. Doesn't matter. I'll take this woman and her sisters on their own merit. We'll see where the friendship leads, or not.*

"Susie and I are interested in taking classes. The *Baywater County Chronicle* article said you'd be starting in January?"

"Yes." Maggie handed a clipboard and pen to Debbie as she explained the questionnaire. "I will email the schedule in late December." She then gave Debbie a quick tour of the shop and the classroom.

"Wow! This is a nice room," Debbie exclaimed.

Ben Davenport had added four windows more than the

single one the original house had offered, as well as installing a door opening to the back porch. Now, plenty of natural light, pure white walls, and two ceiling fans with natural daylight bulbs to offset the dark days, made this room an ideal classroom.

"Tell me, David, how does the chorus go?" Maggie asked after she rang up Debbie's book purchase. David had been whistling the same tune, the *William Tell Overture*, over and over for the past fifteen minutes.

"Huh?" The chair went back onto its four legs without breaking. "Sorry, can't get this tune out of my head."

"You sure got it in mine," his wife answered with a great sigh. "I can do without the Lone Ranger today, or tomorrow. We went to the Masquerade Ball. David was the Lone Ranger, and I was Annie Oakley."

"The original Ranger didn't have a beard," Maggie said to David, smiling.

"Winter's coming on. Wasn't 'bout to shave it off just for that one dance." His voice rose on a querulous note, suggesting his beard may have been fuel for a marital spat prior to the Ball.

After Debbie and David left, Rod came in with the mail. "I picked yours up along with ours," he explained, holding out a Priority Mail envelope first.

Larkin took it from him. "Looks like your friend's book has arrived, too!"

"Go ahead and open it," Maggie said as she sorted through the stack of catalogs and junk mail.

"Oh, what fun! *Splendiferous Bead Motifs!* Imagine making a butterfly with leaf beads and hearts for the wings. And look at the beaded people Sherrill created. And—oh my! This is wonderful!"

Maggie peered over her mother's shoulder. "Think I ought to order a dozen?"

"Two dozen, Maggie dear. This book will surely sell. Oh, look, she autographed it to you. How nice."

Maggie's cell rang. Pattysue had exciting news. Maggie went to the parlor to take the call in private.

"Kaleen called me! She misses me and wants her Teddy. I'm so excited I don't know whether to laugh or cry!"

"Did she tell you where she was?"

"She didn't know. She started to say something, it sounded like 'paw' but she was cut off."

"Mean anything to you?"

"I'm not sure."

"Could she be saying 'paw' for her grandfather?"

"Maybe. Yes! 'Pawpaw' is Paul, my father-in-law."

"Quick, Pattysue, what's Charlotte's cell phone number?"

Pattysue rattled it off while Maggie jotted it down on the message pad. "I'll call the sheriff."

Shortly after Maggie finished talking to the sheriff, Pattysue called back.

"Charlotte just called. Wanted to know what I've been doing. Asked if I heard from Kaleen or her kidnappers yet. I lied and told her I hadn't."

"Pattysue, good for you. I called the sheriff. Walker's on the case, and we'll keep praying that the answers come soon."

*****

A customer came in, shucked off her coat and deposited it in the chair David had just vacated. "Gosh, it's warm in here," she exclaimed. "Unless it's just me."

Maggie checked the thermostat, which was set at a comfortable seventy-two degrees.

The customer picked up a shopping basket and walked over to the sequin display. "I want to embellish this vest. I made it myself. Think these sequin flowers would be big enough to cover the yo-yo centers?"

The yoke of the denim vest was overlaid with yo-yos using the Aunt Gracie thirties' reproduction fabrics. The customer was very proud of her handiwork though it had all the distinctive signs of the "loving hands at home" look. Giving the woman the benefit of the doubt, Maggie suspected that these little gathered circles would be a challenge to make behave and lie flat under the best of circumstances.

"Sequins may not be washable," Maggie cautioned. "You'd best test them first."

"Haven't *you* tested them?" she asked. "You should. It's your job." A serious under bite coupled with the downward trend of her mouth gave the woman a look of perpetual discontent.

Maggie bristled but held her temper.

Larkin interjected, "Most of our customers use sequins on crazy quilts so washing is not an issue."

The yo-yo princess held a package of six-millimeter cupped sequins almost in Maggie's face. "How many sequins in here?"

Maggie backed up. "Five grams."

"How many's that?"

"A bunch." Maggie smiled but her customer scowled. *Maybe she was weaned on pickle juice.*

"Go count them for me!" She shoved the package at Maggie.

Maggie took the package and dropped it in the customer's basket. "No." Her tone would have sent most desperadoes heading for the border. She marched over to stand by the cutting table hoping to curb her rising temper, with Larkin close behind.

CJ and Dart walked in and joined them. "Is she for real?" he asked, *sotto voce*, as he sat down in the visitor's chair.

"Afraid so. I am counting to one thousand, but not sequins," she whispered. "Welcome to the wacky world of retail where the customer is *not* always right."

Dart put his cold nose in her hand. "I know, boy, you're a good pup," she whispered.

"He's taken a strong liking to you already. You're his person now. Joshua will be pleased, too."

The yo-yo princess approached the cash desk. "What's that dog doin' in here? I don't like the looks of him. Dogs belong outside, tied up."

"He's my companion dog. Well trained." She wasn't sure why she even spent the energy to explain Dart to this obnoxious person.

She looked Maggie up and down. "You don't *look* sick," she sneered.

Dart turned around and his ears went forward. She felt him tense and emit a very low rumble. "Dart, easy." The dog with his extra-keen senses didn't like the woman. Maggie sympathized with the dog. She didn't like her either.

"Are you ready to check out?" *Please say you are.*

Oblivious to Maggie's interplay with the dog, the woman set her basket on the counter. It was full of sequins in a variety of sizes along with several tubes of seed beads in different colors. "What thread do I need? Anything special? What size needle will go through these little bitty beads?"

"Silamide thread, made by YLI, is the best. It's strong, resists knotting and fraying. A size eleven straw needle will pass through size eleven seed beads easily."

She opened the tube and extracted one needle. "How do you thread the stupid thing? I cain't even see the hole."

Maggie convinced her to purchase a Bohin super needle-threader after demonstrating its wonderful features.

"Thank you for shopping with us today. Don't forget your coat." *Please, don't forget your coat!*

33

Hog Times Two

AFTER SHE TURNED OFF THE SIGN and locked the front door, Maggie went upstairs to open the kitty doggie-door part of the combination door at the top of the stairs. After hours, she let the feline fur kids out so they could play downstairs.

Propped against the back of the loveseat she found a card from CJ. Just a thinking-of-you card signed with love. *Bless his little Texas-replanted-Yankee heart.* He often left little gifts in odd places to surprise her. A small gold box, holding four exquisite hand-made chocolates from Sweet Things was once found tucked behind the coffee pot. A love note was slipped inside the front cover of the mystery book she was reading at the time. When she least wanted to cook, a hot meal arrived, or he made dinner. She loved the deep shoulder rubs he gave that eased tense muscles. Not much ever ruffled his feathers. An easy soul, a kind man; CJ was a keeper.

At noon, she had put pork tenderloin in the crock-pot. Tonight they would have barbecue pulled pork sandwiches for dinner. The recipe's simple ratio of 2:1:1 was so easy to remember. A two-pound tenderloin, plus one cup each of regular Dr. Pepper and her favorite barbecue sauce, Sweet Baby Ray's. She was thrilled to find that Charlie Baker carried that brand in the Mercantile. Cook on low for four hours. It smelled wonderful already.

Using two wide spatulas she removed the hot tenderloin and set it in a large rectangular glass pan then emptied the cooking liquid out of the crock-pot. As she pulled the tender, aromatic meat apart with two forks, she tossed the shreds back in the empty crock-pot. She poured the remaining barbecue sauce over the shredded meat and stirred it well. It would cook on low for another hour to heat everything up.

Meanwhile, Maggie sat at the kitchen table and sorted through the questionnaires she'd gathered thus far. The requests for beginner classes went in one pile. There were a surprising number who wanted to build onto the basic stitches to create fancy thread-embroidered seams. That, plus silk ribbon embroidery, making ribbon flowers, and bead embroidery were the top four categories. There was enough interest already to start planning for January classes, presuming the weather cooperated, of course.

Stepping through the swinging door of abstraction as she sorted, she wondered how her father-in-law was doing. If she remembered aright, he still lived in the area. It had been a while since she'd called … She glanced at the clock. There was just enough time before dinner to call Emory Blue. Her father-in-law was glad to hear from her. She brought him up to date on her recent activities and inquired about him.

"Doin' all right," he said. "Considering. Laura's been gone five years this month, you know."

"Yes, I did. How's Kerry?" Kerrigan was Kiernan's younger brother, their birthdays a day apart. She'd met Kerry only once, back when she was first dating Kiernan. The brothers looked very much alike except Kerry had a full woodsman's beard back then and Kiernan was clean-shaven.

"He has his ups and downs. Been worse since his mom passed. Have to take him to the VA hospital pretty often. They said it was PTSS or some other alphabet soup name when he first got out of the service. Called it shell-shocked back in my day. Funny how some guys were hit bad. A lot of us were fine, like me. That bike accident he had three years ago, not wearing his dang helmet, really messed up his head. Sometimes he seems like a different person."

PTSS: post-traumatic stress syndrome. Brave men and women face horrors that we at home cannot begin to imagine, comprehend, or fathom, and would rather our valiant troops never had to do so. The human psyche can only take so much abuse before it retreats to protect itself.

Switching to a happier subject, Maggie asked, "What are your Thanksgiving plans, Emory? Same as always?"

"Ayuh. Going to my sister's and her family, I expect. They live up Bangor way. Hope the weather holds."

"You still live in Appleton? I'd like to see you again."

"Ayuh ... but *don't* you come here."

She'd been to their house several times before she married their son. Back roads have changed so much in almost forty years. Trees have grown up in fields that were once all grass. It was hard to recognize even the places she once lived, much less find Emory Blue's house.

"Maybe we could meet at the Sawmill for lunch one of these days soon."

"Maybe. I know, Maggie, I'd like to see you, too. Now's not a good time. Kerry ain't been doin' too well these past couple months. Goes up in the deep woods, all kinds of weather, brooding for hours. Or he stays up all night watching old gangster and western movies. Now, somethin's eatin' at him again."

The sadness and resignation in the old man's voice told a story all its own. Maggie said a silent prayer for her father-in-law's continued health and strength to cope. She checked the clock. Everyone would be here soon so she bid Emory Thanksgiving blessings and journey mercies as they signed off.

She had just put hamburger rolls under the broiler coil when CJ came into the kitchen from the mudroom. Dart ran to greet him, feathery tail a-wagging.

"Is that barbecue pork I'm smelling?"

"It is, and it's very nearly ready."

"Maggie mine, you've stolen my heart."

"I know that, sweetheart. You've got mine, too." She gave him a quick kiss. "Will you get the dill pickles out of the fridge, please?"

"That was a non sequitur if I ever heard one," CJ replied, his words muffled by his head being in the refrigerator.

The distinctive growl of a motorcycle slowing as if it were about to turn onto Cranberry Lane interrupted their happy chatter. It did, and stopped at the mouth of her driveway. Maggie went to the window to watch the biker. Dart put both paws up on the windowsill, watchful and on alert.

The temperature was in the low thirties, yet the biker wore his black bomber jacket wide open, revealing a bad-to-the-bone tee shirt stretched to the limit across his muscled chest. His white-blond hair escaped the red bandana do-rag tied to his head. Lamplight winked at the brass chain attaching his wallet to his belt and glinted off his yellow-tinted glasses.

"This guy must be crazy. No helmet and dressed like that, riding a bike in this weather. CJ, do you know him?" She moved over to the sink and rinsed a plate under the running faucet.

CJ looked out the window where Dart was staying vigilant. "Can't tell. He's too far away, hard to see details in this light. Don't recognize the bike either."

The biker raced the motor, then turned and drove back to Franklin Road.

Rusty jumped up on the sink and stuck his mouth near the running water to get a drink. In doing so, he hit her arm, knocking the wet plate out of her hand. It hit the floor and shattered.

"Are you okay?" CJ joined Maggie at the sink.

"Yes." Maggie got the broom and dustpan out of the broom closet. "This plate sure isn't." She was putting the shards in the wastebasket when the mudroom door opened again.

"Oh, it smells heavenly!" Larkin came in with Rod right behind her. "I brought a buttery lemon cake for dessert."

Maggie looked at the fur trio. Three expectant fuzzy faces all in a row looked up at her.

"*Mff-mee,*" Tuffy's alto sang out.

Rusty added the base tenor note. "*Murp.*"

"*Ruff,*" Dart's deep bass agreed.

"Okay, gang, I hear you! Dinner, coming right up."

Three fur kids! Goes to show you never can tell. In her sweet bungalow in Oklahoma, her only pets were dust bunnies and unicorns, the latter she sometimes tripped over, pesky invisible creatures!

Not counting the surprise visitor she found perched on her living room drape one afternoon at her house in Tucson. The small lizard seemed non-threatening, but until she knew his CV, giving him house privileges had to wait. Sure enough, online, she discovered he was a skink, a benign little creature whose food choice was bugs and other unwelcome-to-her household critters. She gave him *carte blanche* after that. He stayed around about two weeks before he disappeared.

34

Lost and Found

THE BED SHIFTED, BRINGING MAGGIE out of a very deep sleep just enough to be aware of a warm body stretched full out beside her. Turning her head, she went nose to nose with the intruder. Cold. Wet.

Wet? Her eyes popped open.

Dart licked her face, making his message clear. He wanted out. The fur cap on her head was Rusty, dozing with one paw on her forehead. Tuffy was doing aerobic exercises on her stomach, making her want *out* now!

"Okay, everybody. Up and at 'em!"

After disentangling herself from the three-critter congregation, she opened the bedroom door to the upstairs deck for Dart. She heard him thumping back up the metal stairs when she came out of the bathroom.

The rucked-up blanket was evidence that Dart had slept all night in the makeshift bed she'd made for him. She'd promised to get him a nice big wicker doggie bed as soon as possible, hoping the Fur, Feather, and Fin Pet Emporium next door to the veterinarian's office would have one his size.

Dart had already shown her that he did not claim beds or furniture, so he must have been desperate this morning. She had been sleeping so sound that to get her attention he'd leaped up on her bed. It was enough to have the cats hogging the king-sized bed without the dog joining the circus, too. In only two days, she had already learned a lot about the abilities and foibles of this retired K-9 German shepherd addition to her cozy family.

"Breakfast, y'all!" For her own safety's sake, she let the galloping critter trio precede her down the stairs. "No rest for the weary."

The cats were using Dart for a game of leapfrog when she went back upstairs to shower and dress. She decided to leave the gang downstairs today to see how they would interact with customers, if there were any. The dog was of no concern, but she was curious how the cats would cope.

*****

Maggie and Pattysue sat in the classroom, further sorting out the class lists. "Let's separate each group into the days each student prefers. Maybe we'll spot a trend. I'm glad you could work with me today."

Pattysue usually worked for Harold at the Happy Bookworm on Wednesdays. "It was very quiet and my pacing around drove him crazy, so he sent me over here. Anything to keep me busy helps. Oh, I wish we would hear more from K-Kaleen! She sounded so lost and lonesome when she called. I was so excited to hear her voice. But I want my baby back home!"

"It's obvious why Harold sent you to me, my friend." Maggie smiled to take any perceived sting out of her soft-spoken words. "I also enjoy your company, weepy or not." Maggie wrote "Wednesday/bead embroidery" on a pink sticky note.

"How about using a different color sticky note for each day?" Pattysue suggested after blowing her nose.

"Good idea. What did you do last night?" *Besides worry, cry, and pray for your missing daughter.*

"Roy came over, and we made spaghetti. He brought his portable DVD player. We watched an old comedy, *Arsenic and Old Lace,* and a thirties' Jimmy Cagney movie. That was funny, and so hokey! I made popcorn, and we laughed a lot, which helped distract me. Roy even offered to hire a private detective!"

"He cares about you," Maggie agreed. "Though I'm not sure what a PI could do that the sheriff isn't already doing." She picked up the Wednesday/bead embroidery stack, tapped the edges to straighten out the half-sheets and affixed the pink sticky note. She slipped on a paper clip to hold the sheets together.

"I know, but it was sweet of him to offer, just the same." She sniffed and fanned the next stack. "What did you do with the ones who checked off all the boxes?"

"I made photocopies so we could keep them straight this first time out. I'll enter them in the computer before the classes get out of hand. Chances are, I hope, we'll have repeat students."

"This is only for the first quarter so you should have time, especially after the h-holidays." For a moment Pattysue's resolve crumpled. She reached for a tissue, wiped her eyes, and sighed.

"You and Roy have been dating quite a while now, haven't you?"

Pattysue's first meeting with young Dr. Roy Grayson was a date as different as chalk is to cheese. Her husband, Robert Morgan, had blackened her eye, and she'd broken her arm in a fall from the force of the blow. Three days later, she was a widow. Doc took a liking to the young mother and her daughter, so it wasn't long before the friendship blossomed.

The light blush rising on Pattysue's face told Maggie that there was more than simple friendship going on in that twosome.

"Yes. We do something special now and then, just the two of us. Most of the time we go to the museum at the State House, or other fun places. Kaleen loves going with us." Pattysue gulped hard.

"She'll be back with you soon, Pattysue, being just as smart and perky as ever."

"I hope so," she whispered.

There had been one customer first thing this morning and so far, that was it. Maggie decided she'd close the shop next year on Thanksgiving Wednesday, too.

Pattysue's cell phone rang. "No, Roy, nothing … I'll call you, dear, I promise."

To give Pattysue privacy, Maggie ran upstairs to her office to find a pack of multi-colored sticky notes: pink, yellow, green, and blue. A color each for Wednesday through Saturday, and white for the no-date-preference ones. She had no more than sat down at the table when Pattysue's cell phone rang again.

"What?" Pattysue jumped up, scattering the stack of papers in front of her with the sleeve of her sweater. "What'd you say? … The cabin? … I can barely hear you … No, Paul, don't go to my house! I'm at Maggie's! … Come here first." She clicked the phone off and started to bounce up and down before dissolving into tears. "Kaleen's okay! Pawpaw is bringing her home."

"Where is he now? How soon will they get here?" Maggie hugged her young friend, tears of joy coursing down both women's cheeks.

Pattysue let go, grabbed a tissue, and wiped her face. "I don't know, Paul didn't say. Since he was coming from the cabin and it's been snowing hard … He wasn't sure how long it would take him, but he's bringing her here."

CJ hung his coat in the hall closet before joining them in the classroom. "Tonight we're in for a couple inches of snow. It's just starting to come down. Need anything? I'm fixin' to make a run to the Mercantile in a few minutes." He looked at Pattysue who was still laughing and crying at the same time. "Say, what's going on? Good news?"

"Oh, I've got to call Roy back! And my parents, too." Pattysue sprinted to the parlor to call them.

"Quite the best, CJ! Kaleen's safe. Her grandfather is bringing her here," Maggie said. "Let's go to the kitchen and I'll start another pot of coffee."

CJ sat down at the kitchen table. "Does Walker know about this?"

"Does Walker know what?" Sheriff Walker Bainbridge brought a blast of arctic air in with him. Dart went to the big lawman, tail a-wagging, and sniffed his hand. "Hey, big boy, how you doing today?" He leaned down and ruffled the dog's ears. "Keeping those cats in line, are you?"

"The cats are holding their own and so is Dart," Maggie said. "Want coffee?"

At his nod, she poured coffee all around and set a plate of dark chocolate-chocolate chip cookies on the kitchen table.

"The good news is about five minutes old." Maggie said. "Pattysue can tell you more."

After making her phone calls, what little information Pattysue had, she shared with him. "They'll be here soon, I hope. It was hard to hear him through so much static."

"That's great news." Sheriff Bainbridge reached over and patted her hand. "Right after you called me, Maggie, I was finally able to trace Charlotte Morgan's cell. It's in a remote area up in the far northern part of Piscataquis County. It's already two-feet deep and still snowing hard up there. Practically need a dogsled to get in now. This morning the Piscataquis County Sheriff sent out two deputies on snowmobiles to bring her in. She won't be able to drive out of there now."

"That's why Kaleen didn't know where she was," Pattysue explained. "She's never been to their cabin before. On a good day it's a four-five hour drive to that cabin from here. The last bit is most all on secondary and dirt roads."

"I'm surprised there's even cell phone reception that far in," Maggie said.

"Technology is almost everywhere. About four or five miles away is a one-stop-sign town. There's a small grocery store where you can buy gas. There's a cell-phone tower across the road," Pattysue said. "I was only there once, with Bob. Too primitive for me! No electricity or running water. They love to hunt and fish in the summer and early fall. It's not smart to be back there in the boonies this late in the year. I'm surprised Charlee would go there now."

He laid a small plastic bag of beads on the table. "Maggie, tell me about this bracelet."

To better see the beads, she pressed the plastic down around them with both hands. "Wow! The large faceted ones are vintage Swarovski crystal bi-cones. See the intense sparkle? It's the high lead content in the glass that makes them so pretty. There are crystal beads out there with a lower lead content, made in China, Japan, Taiwan, and India. They don't have the sparkle, the reflective quality found in Swarovski crystals." She patted the plastic again trying to see the spacer beads.

"The little bitty beads are called Charlottes. A facet has been cut on one face of the seed bead. Depending on where the facet is oriented when the light hits, it causes random sparkles. Too bad the clasp is broken. Wait a minute! Something's engraved on the back of the clasp. Initials ... CBM."

"That's Charlotte's bracelet! Charlotte Brock Morgan," Pattysue exclaimed.

"Where'd you find this, Walker?" Maggie asked the sheriff.

"Harold found it. This morning he was sweeping out from under the stack over by where Tony Leblanc's body was found. He saw something sparkle and called me immediately."

"Wasn't Charlotte wearing a similar matching necklace and bracelet the day you two had lunch here?" Maggie asked Pattysue.

"Yes ... yes, she was. Charlee always wears glitzy jewelry. She has sets in several different colors. When Kaleen was little, she loved to play with Cha-Cha's bracelet." Pattysue blanched. "Are you saying Charlee ... killed ... T-Tony?"

The sheriff did not answer her question. "Does she wear red fuzzy wool gloves?"

"Y-yes. I gave them to her for Christmas last year."

Dart sighed. He had his head on his paws, half asleep. Tuffy was snug up beside him with one little white paw on the dog's left paw. Rusty was draped across the dog's back.

"They are getting along fine. And I'm in love with all three of them." She shot CJ a look. "And no more kids, okay?"

Walker Bainbridge's head swiveled back and forth between Maggie and CJ. He shrugged his massive shoulders, smoothed his luxuriant handlebar mustache, and chuckled. "Let me know when they get here. I need to run an errand for Abigail, then I'll be back."

"We have quite a crowd coming to Eagles' Rest tomorrow. How about you?"

He stood up, preparing to leave. "There's a big to-do at Abigail's mother's house in Augusta. Kith, kin, in-laws, outlaws, cousins, and strays. The usual motley crew."

Right after CJ went out with Maggie's shopping list in hand, the front door opened, admitting several customers who came in together. Maggie told Pattysue to stay put then shut the Dutch door to the kitchen and went to help the four women. Two hours and a thousand dollars in sales later, Maggie turned off the Open sign. That big sale made it worth being open after all, but she was thankful to be closing early. She had pies to make and things to prepare for tomorrow, not to mention what to have for supper tonight when everyone gathered here for the pie-baking marathon.

CJ returned with several large shopping bags and, bless him, put her groceries away.

"That place was a madhouse. Not as young as I used to be," he moaned, rubbing his lower back.

"Are you saying you're ancient?" Maggie teased as she brought a large block of cheddar cheese out of the refrigerator.

"I'm four years older than you, so I'm getting older faster than you." CJ took a large knife out of the drawer.

Maggie handed CJ a maple cutting board. "Positively ancient!" she said with a tinge of deviltry in her tone.

"Define ancient." He peeled the plastic wrap off the cheese.

"Someone who shouldn't sit in profile to have a silhouette cut, or to be photographed." She ran her hand down her chin to her still-firm neck. Slender, five-nine, and blessed with good genes, she doubted she'd ever have to deal with a double chin in her fast-increasing double-digit years. "Silhouettes are so out of vogue now, but even back in the day, the best ones were of children and young people."

"Like Alfred Hitchcock's famous profile? Big belly, pout, and all."

"Quite. Slice this cheddar, please, not too thick. It's for sandwiches." Along with the sandwiches they would have homemade tomato soup for supper tonight, after everyone arrived. Time was now wandering past three-thirty and the sun, what there was of it, was already making haste westward to bid this day good-bye.

CJ chopped onions while Maggie opened three large cans each of diced tomatoes, three of tomato puree, and two regular size cans of tomato sauce. She dumped them in a big kettle with two tablespoons of sugar to offset the acid of the tomatoes, two tablespoons of Italian mixed herbs, a tiny dollop of garlic, and the chopped onions.

As she set the kettle on the back burner to simmer she heard a car pull off onto Cranberry Lane. She looked out the kitchen window. "They're here!"

A red Jeep crept in the driveway and came to a slow stop beside the porch. An old man got out then reached in to pick up a small child. He staggered up the steps, carrying her. Maggie opened the front door. Pattysue, with tears running down her face unchecked, ran past and took her daughter from him.

CJ was calling Sheriff Walker Bainbridge when the weary travelers stumbled into the warm kitchen. He appropriated Pattysue's house keys and went to fetch Teddy and pajamas for the little girl.

35

Safe!

PATTYSUE SAT IN THE GLIDER ROCKER cradling her sleepy-eyed daughter, smelling of roses-and-cream bath soap. The child wore pink-poodle flannel pajamas and clutched her much-loved bear in a death grip.

Paul Morgan slumped in the wing chair. His features were gray and drawn making him appear much older than his seven decades on earth should show. His voice often faltered while he told the sad story.

Walker Bainbridge had brought a voice recorder with him. Paul Morgan agreed to have his statement recorded. "I only want to say this once, Sheriff."

Maggie and CJ served mugs of coffee, hot chocolate, or tea as people expressed their preferences. They gathered around and listened.

"Charlotte assured me she had permission to have Kaleen for a week. Sunday, she announced that we would go up to our cabin. The weather report looked good, at least for a couple of days anyway. I was a little surprised Pattysue agreed, especially this close to Thanksgiving. She's been standing up for herself more lately. But Charlotte always manages to get her way.

"Poor little Kaleen kept asking for Teddy. She fussed

that she didn't say goodbye to Mommy. She never went overnight anywhere without that bear. Those two things got me wondering if Charlotte was telling me the truth."

Paul asked his daughter-in-law, "She asleep?"

Pattysue looked down. "Sound asleep."

"Good. She doesn't need to hear this. Charlotte kept her cell phone turned off. She said it was 'to save the battery' but that was right after she caught Kaleen 'playing' with her phone yesterday. That little girl isn't stupid. I bet she tried to call you, Pattysue."

"She did, Paul, but was cut off before she could say much."

"After that, Charlotte called someone, but who it was, I don't know. A minute later it rang. I thought it was Pattysue from what Charlotte was saying."

"Do you remember what time that was?" the sheriff asked.

"I think it was right after lunch."

"That's when Maggie called me. That was the break we needed and we were able to trace the location of Charlotte's phone," the sheriff said.

"You should have tried mine. I keep it on all the time," Paul said.

"I forgot you had one, Paul. I'm sorry." Kaleen stirred, and Pattysue dropped her voice. "I don't know your number anyway."

Paul smiled at her and also lowered his voice. "Later, I overheard Charlotte telling Kaleen that her mommy didn't love her as much as we did. We needed a little girl because we didn't have one. Charlotte was determined to have Kaleen, one way or another. Kept insisting the child was better off with us since she didn't have a daddy now. We could do so much more for her.

"Last night, Charlotte said that we would leave the cabin tomorrow, uh, today, and head over to New Hampshire." He pulled off his glasses and rubbed his sleep-deprived eyes.

"That scared me. She does have a younger sister in Portsmouth, but she was too vague about it. That's crossing state lines with a small child. Something just didn't feel right. I told her I wouldn't go along with it. We argued, upsetting Kaleen. I finally got the child calmed down and back to bed." He replaced his glasses and yawned.

"Charlotte rushed into our bedroom. She lit a kerosene lamp then opened the drawer in the bedside table where she keeps a Lavender Lady .38 Special. I was right behind her when she pulled out the gun, swiveled around and pointed it at me. I had only one option, Sheriff. I took her out with a sucker punch to the jaw. I've never hit a woman before. Desperate times mean desperate measures." He pulled a rumpled handkerchief out of his pocket and blew his nose.

"I took her gun with me. Didn't trust my wife not to do something stupid. It was almost midnight. I closed the bedroom door and put the lamp on a small stool in the front room. It's mighty dark out there at midnight. I wrote a note saying I'd be back tomorrow ... today ... to get her. I bundled the child up. We'd no sooner gotten out on the porch when a gust of wind yanked the door away from me and slammed it so hard I felt the cabin shake." He took a deep breath before continuing the saga.

"The roads were terrible and getting worse by the minute. In places, I had to crawl along, even in four-wheel drive, praying I wouldn't go off the road. It was snowing so bad it was hard to make out where the edge of the road ended and the ditch began. When I got to the main highway, it was a little easier going. I followed the snowplow all the way in."

Pattysue struggled to stand up. Kaleen was sound asleep in her mother's arms.

"Sit still. I'll get her." CJ got out of his chair and picked up the limp child, still clutching Teddy. He laid her on the small couch with the bear and tucked Dotty's colorful afghan around them.

Pattysue moved to sit on the arm of her father-in-law's chair. She hugged him. "It's okay, Paul. Kaleen's safe now, and so are you."

"Oh, Pattysue, you are such a blessing to me." He grabbed her hand and held it for several minutes before he continued. "I am so sorry this happened. I love that little girl ... and you, too. You were too good for that sorry so-and-so. I'm going to make it up to you. I want to set up a living trust for both of you, to pay for her education, and whatever else you and she ever need in this world."

The sheriff's cell phone rang. He went to the hall to take the call. In a few minutes he returned, looking grim.

"I'm sorry. It's not good news. The deputies made it to your cabin." He laid his big hand on the old man's shoulder. "It's burnt to the ground. There is a fatality."

"Oh. Charlotte," he moaned. "Where ... did you find ... her?"

"On the floor in the bedroom. When the deputies finally got there, there was hardly anything left. The smoke got her before the fire did. She never knew what happened, Mr. Morgan. I'm so sorry."

Paul buried his face in his work-hardened hands. His sigh seemed to come all the way from his lace-up leather boots. "What's meant to be will always find a way. I guess it's as it should be. The gun is locked in the glove box. I suspect you'll want it, Sheriff. Charlotte told me she'd shot Tony— but it was a mistake. From behind, Harold and Tony are about the same build."

"Merciful heavens," Maggie exclaimed. "She really meant to kill Harold!"

36

Un-Sweet Charlotte

"I THINK WE BETTER GET HAROLD OVER HERE. He may have some answers for us," the sheriff said as he dialed the number.

About fifteen minutes later Harold Tottenbaum was sitting in the kitchen. He paled when he learned about Charlotte Morgan's death, which did not escape the sheriff's keen eyes.

"Why would Charlotte want to kill you?"

"Me? After all this time? That happened back in high school."

Harold was not stupid. By his expression of dawning comprehension, he knew what the sheriff was after. "Charlotte was in the bookstore one day last summer, telling a friend about how she, Charlotte, was going after custody of Kaleen. I told her I would testify against her and bring up the old scandals to show she was too unstable to care for the child."

"Aha, that's what I overheard at the Depot, but it made no sense to me then," Maggie said. "Oops, you said scandals? Plural?"

"It's a long story. Charlotte Brock and I went to high school together. Winter break, several of us went skiing. I had been dating Emily, her younger sister. Charlotte wanted us to break up so she could date me, and I refused." He paused and asked Maggie for a glass of water.

"She hated her little sister. Emily usurped Charlotte's place in the family dynamics. Emily was prettier, sweeter, smarter, and became her daddy's little princess. Charlotte was insanely jealous and played nasty tricks on Emily. Emily always forgave her big sister, which infuriated Charlotte." He finished the water and shifted sideways in the wooden chair.

"Emily was new to skiing so she was using a pair of borrowed skis. Before we went out that second morning, I saw Charlotte fussing with the bindings. Her back was to me, so I couldn't see exactly what she was doing. Out on the slopes, Emily took a turn too hard, lost her ski and ran headfirst into a tree. Broke her neck. She died instantly. The county sheriff said four of the screws that hold the binding on were loose and let go under torque. That's next to impossible to have one screw loose, much less four, even if the skis were old. The sheriff was suspicious of Charlotte but had no hard evidence to prove it was anything other than an unfortunate accident."

"Did Charlotte think that with Emily out of the way, you would date her?" Maggie asked.

"Yes. When I refused, and told her why, she's hated me ever since."

"What was the second incident?" the sheriff asked.

"She ended up married to another one of our classmates, Jim Daly. They had a baby, Robert. A couple years later, Jim died of food poisoning. Charlotte was sick, but not to the degree that Jim was. She'd made a turkey casserole, which I know Jim loved. He'd rave about his wife's turkey casserole. He must have eaten a full plateful. By the time Charlotte called for help, it was too late for Jim. The doctor had his suspicions, but he couldn't prove it. Charlotte took the baby and moved to Camden where no one knew her."

"It only takes a tiny bit of spoiled turkey to set off a violent reaction," Maggie said with a shudder. Many years ago, she and a friend had gone out to dinner the Monday following Thanksgiving. The turkey tasted off and had a pink cast to it. One bite was all she ate. It was enough. She was sick for three days.

"I met her at an ice cream place. We hit it off and got married. I adopted her son; he was such a cute little feller," Paul Morgan said. "I never heard any of this before. She hardly ever said anything about her past."

"I don't think she'd want to brag about it," Maggie said.

"I always believed she poisoned Jim."

"Why, Harold?" Maggie asked.

"Jealousy in its vilest incarnation, and revenge. Jim was pulling away from her. After he died, I still refused to date her. I was married to my dear Mary then. I never saw Charlotte again until after Kaleen was born." He sighed. "I doubt Charlotte would have hurt Kaleen. At least until she was a teenager, attracting boys, and defecting by taking her affections elsewhere."

37

Pie-Baking Marathon

THE DOWN-HOME SMELL OF PUMPKIN PIES baking filled the Cottage's kitchen. Maggie made the piecrusts and lined the pie pans. Damia filled them with the pecan pie mixture that Larkin had made.

CJ was peeling apples. As the bowl was filling up, Pattysue dusted the apple slices with a sifted mixture of sugar and spices. Two of the apple pies would have sun-dried cranberries and walnuts added.

Maggie had made grilled cheese sandwiches, and Pattysue dished up tomato soup for everyone before they started the assembly line for pies. Four of each kind assured that tomorrow's diners would not miss out on their favorites, that is, if they had any room left for dessert!

Joshua, Rod, Harold, and Paul stayed out of the way, talking cars, fishing, books, and whatnot in the parlor. The cats were upstairs, out from under foot. Dart was camped beside Joshua's chair, also staying out of the bustle in the kitchen.

The pumpkin pies were done and cooling on the counter. Next up were the pecan pies.

"It's getting late, Maggie. I'll take the apple pies home to bake them there," Larkin insisted.

After Rod and Larkin departed, everyone else was gathered around the kitchen table savoring cups of hot chocolate when Pattysue's cell phone rang.

"That was Cooper, wishing us a happy Thanksgiving. He won't be joining us after all. Seems he found a former classmate online. They met and hit it off, so he's spending the day with her in Kennebunkport. Oh, I almost forgot to tell you! I'm going to have a baby sister! My mom and dad are adopting a small child. She's part French and Abenaki. Her name is Matilda Rosebud."

"Congratulations. How fun!" Maggie hugged her young friend.

"Well, at least those two mysteries are solved." Joshua wiped the marshmallow mustache from his own mustache.

38

Waxing Poetic

IT WAS VERY LATE, BUT MAGGIE SAT on the loveseat in the sitting room thumbing through today's mail. With all the excitement of Kaleen's return, supper with so many friends crowded around the kitchen table, adding the hubbub of assembly line pie baking, she hadn't paid any attention to it. Everybody was gone now, so quiet reigned. The three fur-kids were in their respective beds. Well, more to the point, Dart was stretched out in *his* new wicker doggie bed while both cats were asleep on *her* pillow.

The familiar handwriting on the bright blue envelope caused her to smile. She opened the letter and read:

> *My dear friend,*
>
> *In one breath I could say I am envious that you are living your dream by a lake in Maine while I remain in winds-across-the-plains Oklahoma. In the very next breath I will say how truly glad I am for you. A verse in Philippians behooves us to be content, more or less to bloom where we are planted. Each of us is where she belongs, and where we each need to be.*
>
> *Ages ago I wrote a poem about being home-*

sick at Christmas. It will be included in a collection of short stories and poems that will be out in a few months. You, special friend of mine, are getting a sneak preview.

I miss you. Remember, though, if we don't see each again on this earth, as we now know it, I'll see you on the Other Side.

Joy, peace, and More Beyond!

Hugs, Sherrill

Another paper was tucked behind this short note. It was winter snow scene stationery on which the poem was printed.

39

Homesick

HOME FOR CHRISTMAS

"If wishes were horses," a friend asked of me,
"Home for Christmas, where would that special heart place
be?"
No strings attached, dream however I might,
Home for Christmas, that place came easy to my mind's
sight.

The cabin waited far back on the land
Surrounded by cedars, verdant sentinels, stately and grand.
Snowflakes waltzed in the arms of the drifter.
The west wind sighed, its ethereal music carried in a whis-
per.

Moon slice, sliver thin, pale light aglow
Made fairy diamonds glitter in the blanket of new-fallen
snow.
Across the midnight canvas, brave clouds scudded by,
Cast shadows, patched and strange, imagination on the fly!

Sherrill M. Lewis

A frisky breeze skipped past my front door.
A feathery wave sent a whisper of sea foam to kiss the shore.
Century-strong walls the vagrant winter shuns.
Cozy and safe inside, I'll take my rest, day's wandering
    done.

Home for Christmas: my heart's peace to regain.
A cottage by the sea where I'll bolt my wandering in,
    Downeast in Maine.
The homesick heart cries out, sorrow sung in a minor key,
For the dream is fleeting. Right now, Oklahoma is home for
    me.

Home for Christmas: fond memories to hang your hat on.
It's an old, old Story written by Matthew, Mark, Luke, and
    John.
Jesus' birthday. He lived. He died. He rose again. My heart
    sings!
I believe, so I'll be Home for Christmas forever, with the
    King of Kings!

40

Thanksgiving

EXTRA LEAVES HAD BEEN ADDED to the dining room table to accommodate the eighteen people, resplendent in their casual evening wear, gathered for Thanksgiving dinner at Eagles' Rest. The lace tablecloth was snowy white, the crystal sparkled, the silver gleamed, and the large antique oak buffet cabinet groaned.

Rod, with Larkin at his right, sat at the head of the oval table while CJ sat at the opposite end with Maggie at his right.

Dart was camped under Maggie's chair. Though they'd made friends earlier with the new dog, Siam and Sheba were secluded in the spacious utility room during dinner.

Joshua and Damia claimed seats beside Maggie, while everyone else seemed to migrate wherever they pleased. Maggie looked around the table. Maisie and Terrance O'Reilly, Artesia and Rossiter Lovington, Dotty Thystleberry, Harold Tottenbaum, Dorothea Sanger, Elda Carmichael, and Paul Morgan. Little Kaleen Morgan sat between Dr. Roy Grayson and Pattysue Morgan.

They held hands around the table while Rod said grace and a prayer for peace and love to blossom within this circle. Plates were laden down and the chatter around the table was lively in between bites and singing the praises of the cooks who had contributed to the feast.

CJ said, "I'm curious, Rod and Joshua, why neither of you went for higher ranks than Colonel. You were both career military."

"In the Air Force, a Brigadier General is the next higher rank. It's a long, involved process where a board of general officers creates a list of candidates. The President then chooses the ones to be promoted from that pool. The kicker was I had to retire after thirty years of service or after five years in that rank. Larkin and I decided to stay where I was. We were happy, and that's what matters."

"What about you, Joshua?"

"I was involved in certain work that to advance would have cramped my ability to function as freely and covertly as I needed, and as my country also needed me. Besides, I made Miss Maggie a solemn promise. And I never break my promises."

"Your friendship has been a blessing for me, brother man."

"What? *Has been*? I'm not done yet, *boo*."

"I stand corrected! Still *is* a blessing, Joshua, with you and Damia both. I'm not done yet, either."

Maggie noticed that Harold and Dotty had struck up quite an energetic discussion about books. They both looked delighted to find themselves sitting next to another bibliophile. Dorothea Sanger, who was one of the staunch Library Friends, sat on Harold's right. She added a third lover of books into the happy conversation.

Ross Lovington leaned forward. "You got the hat and the

boots, Dubois. You got cattle?"

Maggie tensed. Ross's tone said he had no use for tin-horn Saturday-night cowboys. CJ did not look aggrieved with the man's no-holds-barred question, so she relaxed.

"Got a few. Rockin' Diamond D's main focus is horses," CJ answered, matching Ross's pistols-at-twenty-paces stare.

A few? I guess a hundred head of beef cattle might be "few" by Texas standards.

"Well, now, I reckon I know the brand. Good stock," Ross Lovington told CJ, warming up at the recognition. "Last of our ranchin' days, I only had a thousand head of cattle. We raised thoroughbreds, too, till I struck oil. Turned the ranch over to our oldest daughter, but I kept the oil rights. Never looked back." He drained his wine glass and set it down.

"We raise a few thoroughbreds for certain customers. Our best horses are the easy-riding Tennessee Walkers," CJ said.

Maggie swallowed a forkful of sweet potato casserole. "Not familiar with that breed. Most horses I've ever ridden were anything *but* easy. I rode every chance I got, which wasn't often enough for me. I loved horses almost as much as my guitar."

Rod interjected, "I read a quote the other day by Ian Fleming you may appreciate. 'A horse is dangerous at both ends and uncomfortable in the middle.' Sounds like some of your equine experience, m'dear."

"You've never ridden a Tennessee Walker." CJ wiped runaway gravy off his chin.

"Would I have found that much of a difference if I had?"

Maggie buttered a still-warm yeast roll.

"Oh, yes, *querida*. When you come down to the Rockin' Diamond D, I'll put you on Smoke. He's the smoothest, easiest-riding horse I ever slapped a saddle on."

"Rocking-chair smooth, sweetheart? I'm too old to ride, I fear. My hips would not be happy. I'd be spending a lot of time in a *wooden* rocking chair, hopefully well padded."

"We've got those, too. Wide porch hugs right up to the front door, begging to have rocking chairs on it, and we do. Six of 'em."

At the lull following dessert, Roy Grayson got up and stood behind Kaleen's chair. He proposed a toast, thanking the Richardsons for opening their home for today's celebration. Then with a cat-and-canary grin, he opened a black velvet ring box and removed a diamond ring. It caught the light from the chandelier and returned the sparkle of a thousand rainbows. He slipped it on Pattysue's finger. Cheers went up and Pattysue blushed. Kaleen clapped and squealed with delight. Paul Morgan, looking much healthier after a decent night's sleep, slapped Roy on the back, offering his heartiest congratulations.

*****

CJ held Maggie's chair for her then tucked her arm in his. He led her to the far corner of the Lake Room and kissed her. "Before it gets crowded in here, I want to know something."

"What?"

In the background came the soulful sound of Percy Sledge's classic song: *"When a man loves a woman ..."*

He handed her a small blue velvet box. "If you like this." As she began to open it he said, "Maggie mine, marry me."

She looked at the three square-cut diamonds in a white gold fancy filigree setting. "Oh!"

He slipped the ring on her finger as she spoke the words she was very ready to say. "Yes, CJ, I will marry you."

Stay in touch! There's more to come!

Sherrill M. Lewis

Recipe: Sherrill's
"Not Your Mama's Mac & Cheese!"

½ pound (2 cups raw) elbow macaroni (makes 5 cups cooked) *Note: Any other pasta may be substituted as long as you end up with 5 cups of cooked pasta.*
Cook macaroni in boiling water for 7-10 minutes.
Drain and return to pan; cover to keep warm.

Butter a 9"x13" baking pan; set aside.

In large bowl, combine:
> 3 eggs, whisked until frothy
> ½ stick (4 tablespoons) butter, melted
> ¼ cup shredded mozzarella cheese
> 1½ cups half & half (or whole milk)
> A pinch each of salt and black pepper (optional)

Add this mixture to warm macaroni.
Stir until cheese is melted and mixture is reasonably smooth.

Add to macaroni and stir well:
> 2½ cups Mexican Fiesta shredded cheese mix [Fiesta contains Monterey Jack, Cheddar, Queso Quesadilla, and Asadero.]
> 1 cup Kraft shredded cheese mix, [mix contains: Parmesan, Romano, and asiago]

Pour mac & cheese into prepared pan. Sprinkle ½ cup (or more!) of Fiesta cheese mix on top of pasta.

Bake in 375° oven for 15-20 minutes, until cheese is golden brown.

Sherrill M. Lewis

The Author

SHERRILL M. LEWIS IS A SELF-TAUGHT ARTIST across diverse media. Since her senior year in high school, she has won awards for writing, art dolls, beadwork, crazy quilts, and photography. In 2010, her first technique-oriented book, *Splendiferous Bead Motifs!*, was published. In 2014, *Uncultured Pearl*, her first novel in the Maggie Storm Blue Mystery Series, was published. She has now published her second (*Deadly Chevrons*) and third (*Deadly Facets*) books in the Series. Raised in Maine, she currently resides on an idyllic, never boring, five acres in Payne County, Oklahoma, with her husband Gene.

Photo by Karen Lemley © 2003